MW01087520

Three Goat Songs

Michael Brodsky

Other books by
Michael Brodsky
available from
Four Walls Eight Windows

Xman

(cl): $21.95

(pb): $11.95

X in Paris

(pb): $9.95

Dyad

(cl): $23.95

(pb): $11.95

Three Goat Songs

Michael Brodsky

Four Walls Eight Windows | **New York**

Published by:

Four Walls Eight Windows
PO Box 548
Village Station
New York, NY, 10014

First edition.
First printing April 1991.

Library of Congress Cataloging-in-Publication Data:

Brodsky, Michael, 1948—
ISBN 0-941423-46-8 (cl.)/ISBN: 0-941423-47-6 (pbk.)
I. Title
PS3552.R6233T47   1991   90-49706
813'.54—dc20   CIP

Printed in the U.S.A.

Text designed by Chris Wise.

What point, amid still another circle of rehabilitators, in running their stipulated gauntlet of admission to every conceivable rancor and rage without the gauziest pledge of some answering intention to construct, and from just such shards, that anti-totality exclusively equipped to squelch its metastasizing double insidiously touted as—the self, perfectible at last.

Goat Song 1

Not a particularly long time was required to discover their symptoms were opposed. She had a predilection for well-fed goats whereas he was drawn toward the mineral, or rather, whenever it was a question of the mineral and nothing but the mineral very quickly it became a sliding toward total dispossession.

More accurate to say her predilection was anticipatory horror in the face of his inevitable surrender to their charms. No point in telling her he positively loathed goats, well fed or not: Her symptom had already learned to be intolerant of the specifications of his own: His symptom was inconceivable to her own, which had its own course to run and intended to run it.

Each time they went out, with or without the little ones, into the sunny seaside air she tormentedly hammered out her symptom into a statement to the effect that now for the last time only did she need to be told he would never abandon her for a well-fed goat. How explain that this presentation of still another request for reassurance as the absolutely very last request was but the surest perpetuation of such requests.

Sometimes he was amused by the way she clutched at his wrist when a well-fed goat descended the steeps before them in the direction of the sea. Or rather, affected in some way by her clutching he chose or was compelled to call the affection amusement. She was forever on the lookout for udders wriggling amid the offal heaps adjacent to their home ground. Sometimes he caught sight of a goat long before her but made it his business to turn away, pretending not to have seen. Though it could be hard pretending with the animal busy urinating all over its beard. At any rate, *busy* was not the right word since in such cases the animal was invariably distracted by an odor of alfalfa, or timothy, or peanuts, or sudan grass emanating from a nearby browse. His momentary vision of himself—in her—in somebody's—vision—as one who had missed a goat, did not care enough for the goats of this world not to miss a goat—filled him with momentary delight. At once he became the innocent her—somebody's—mistake made him out to be.

When sucking at the surface of the mineral world he was also innocent—but only in her unseeing presence. In that presence the sucking did not register as anything but laudable nonsurrender to the

1

goats. Outside her presence his connection to the mineral world could only assume a somber canted unspeakableness. And there was no emptying it out, this connection, this unspeakable connection, it was always regenerated. Rather, connection or retreat from connection was always different. Rather, he who worked hard to work himself up to believing that talk about the connection would be equivalent to a being cured of said connection found that the connection was always taking new forms that invalidated, rendered completely irrelevant, any previous saying about the connection—had there been any such saying. What began over and over to smell like an outworn and unfashionable connection exhausted by the words he one day anticipated speaking suddenly revealed itself as the newest of new connections, albeit at the very heart of the old connection, clearly subsumed by the old yet completely new. Of course all this made sense only within walking distance of a confessor. But he wanted to steer clear of confessors for in actual fact he did not want to tell his confession. Without ever having known confessors already he had had more than his fill of the subspecies. With such a connection at his fingertips there could never come a time when he need fear no longer shocking the ever delicate sensibilities of the confessor he abjured with all his heart and soul.

For example, a sudden penchant for an upsurge of rock right at the water's edge—an upsurge flayed by tiny lichenlike hairs of the same fulvous or gamboge as the fissure whence they grew—the rawness of this penchant made all previous avowal irrelevant, beggared all previous exorcism. For here was a version of the symptom undeducible from and insusceptible to the reassurances appropriate to any prior avowal. Here at last was a version of the symptom—the connection—for which there never could be words, a category for which all words found could only qualify as the easiest camouflages to sleight of hand, as cunning makeshifts not only duping confessor but cutting off speaker from perpetual tangency to the intrinsic unsayability—that is, the very heart, the very soul—of the connection. He was learning that once he found himself talking about the connection he could be sure he was no longer in, of, the connection.

Yet even if not to a confessor sometimes he had a hunger to rehearse the addiction—this was what it was—to, for example, the tiny hairs that striped the smooth rock faces smoothed even further by spume there where the incoming tide was briniest. She did not care. It was his—in her eyes overriding—craving for the well-fed goats, able to prink and preen in a manner impossible for one whose life was as difficult as hers—it was his overriding penchant for the goats—so hypnotizing and against whose charms he was axiomatically power-less—that concerned her. Pretending to take her madness seriously as they were returning at dusk with the little ones after a visit to the old folks he insisted it was still not clear whether he was charmed by the goats themselves or simply overwhelmed by, appropriated to, their desire for him, which appropriation, he might add, obliterated and rendered laughable any question of an answering desire. Her worry was all he got for answer.

Off he would go, whenever he got the chance, or made the chance, far from goats and rocks, collapsing in a blind field spangled with horseflies. In vain he tried to daydream, about a particularly enticing rock face, about what life might be like unburdened by rock faces or rather connection with rock faces or by the reproaches of a yokemate convinced of his connection with goats—in vain he tried to pursue these lines of thought. For they always converged on the same fantasy: Spotting him from a distance routing among his byproducts here she was descending to be sure of catching him in the act. And what was her surprise when she found him all alone, entertaining neither goats nor lichen-encrusted rock fissures, not that she would have balked at his entertaining lichen though strictly speaking she could be aban-doned in the name of lichens as well as of goats. But for her there was abandonment and then there was abandonment and abandonment in behalf of lichens did not have the same tonality as abandonment in the name of goats. Seeing himself through her eyes as she advanced upon him—more than exonerated, exalted in his innocence—completely in-capable of deciphering the urgency of such an advance—this was the image to which he over and over again returned.

One day as they were sitting at the edge of the road and at the very moment when she was about to speak of their future a flock of well-fed goats approached, slueing more than they scurried, even if scurrying was in fact their prime function. She clutched his arm. In

3

response he said he had absolutely no interest in goats. She nodded: You say that but deep down. He cut her off, though she had already cut herself off. He felt the upsurge of an exultation at the prospect of now shocking, now reassuring her: I cannot conceive of myself not loving smooth fissured rock faces streaked with fine hairs. And as he spoke something new dawned on him: I mean, once I perceived such a craving could exist I could not conceive of not being saddled with such a craving. She tilted her face. This meant: How did you learn of such a craving. This meant: With what kind of foul company were you obliged to consort to end up learning of such a craving. Proudly he replied, I learned of it from myself and myself alone, with all due respect, that is, for the hysteresis between the learning and the craving when said craving is, so to speak, just a craving to skirt the boundaries of such a craving. Taxing her perplexed impatient eagerness for him to continue he did indeed continue but as he went about continuing he realized the signal to continue came not singly from her but from their—his and her—collusion with the impatient eagerness of the landscape, rocks and all: It seemed inconceivable that I should not be saturated with such a craving—tainted by such a craving—for to be saddled with such a craving is to be connected to nonbeing, is to not be. Whereas the craving—the symptom—the hunger—the connection you saddle me with—the craving your symptom decrees that I am to be saddled with belongs to the far larger domain of the comprehensible and makes me member of a community to which I do not wish to belong. Maybe I belonged to it once, maybe never. Seeing her weep I relented, adding: The only problem is I can't decide whether I developed the craving without exposure to outside influence or stumbled upon it in the wilderness. No matter the provenance: suffice it to say I have developed this unappeasable craving for the melancholy ruthlessness of smooth rock faces and in a spasm appropriating it—the craving—have kept it warm inside me ever since. Yet even though I am one with my craving—whenever I see outside me configurations in any way resembling the configurations that effected the initial appropriative spasm I cannot help feeling what I see miraculously mimics, coincides with, what after all has been incontrovertibly born deep within, has its roots, its origin, deep within that within. She said, obviously still intent on the goats: Yes, how explain the craving born from within but not the target of the craving. How explain the target of the craving being contaminated by, assimilated to, the autochthonousness of the mother craving. He mused: For all practical purposes they too—the rock faces—are now autochthonous to my depths. He tried to explain how he was still dully wondering that anything in the outside world should end up resembling, would dare to resemble, those spiky sullen forms germinated—proposed from—within. Her sidelong look told him clearly he had forgotten that it was in the outside world he was first schooled in these—his—forms and in how to excruciate along the contour of such forms. And so my wonderment, he retorted, stunned and spasmed surprise, that such forms can exist out there, in perfect mimicry of those within, perfections long incubated with no help from the outside world, this stunned surprise has become in fact, according to you, my desire, my craving, my symptom. I don't hunger—always according to you—after the rock faces themselves but after their blatant daring to be identical with precursors living, lived, within. She looked pained, not so much for herself as for meaning. For such a construction defaced the halidom of meaning as she recalled it from her last stint of consecration. For here was meaning no longer determining the trajectory of words required to capture it but itself forced to yield to the caprice of their convulsed proliferative inbreeding.

In other words, he went on, even if she was once again living only for the receding buttocks of the goats or their advancing udders, my desire, my hunger, my craving, my connection is nothing more than my astonishment that the archetypes of that desire—that hunger, etc., can subsist as run-of-the-mill ectypes. Then vindictively, as if to stump and do him in for overpopulating her life with goats and rocks when all she had ever really wanted, etc.: And what is the connection between finding it inconceivable that you should not love these hairy-fissured spume-spluttered rock faces and finding it inconceivable that these very rock faces may be found without the incubation of the eternally postponed possibility of their manifestation sometime in the near future? Or was she shaming his failure to generate another meaning of the sort that had just capsized defaming her long cherished conception of meaning? Was she developing a craving for just this sort of meaning? Everything went blurry, bloody. He looked at her, hurt, not so much at her asking the question as at her asking it here and now, at this point, of such evident vulnerability and bloody, blurry confusion. He would have preferred her asking later on, when the question could be linked if not to an answer then to some equally potent counterquestion capable of defusing its potency. This was a question outside their story, a question aimed at his depths that had no business being mixed up with the story as he intended to contour its unfolding, shear its multiplication. All he could think of in the way of answer was: Sometimes I pretend I don't love the rocks, their smooth unwrinkled recession from my drunken touch. Sometimes I tell myself I am still making up my mind about their faces. But before I can begin to make up my mind about whether or not to make up my mind I find myself actively inventorying, absorbing eagerly through such inventory, certain . . . secondary sexual characters perceptible to and inventoriable by only a seasoned aficionado. Before I have made up my mind whether or not to offer habitation to the craving—the desire—the hunger—the symptom, it has already taken up residence and more than residence, has gone ahead and eaten up too too many qualia—golden ears of wheat on a swaying boulder, for example—to allow my wavering any credibility.

He looked out to sea and hoped his apparent reflective calm would shame her into calm too. After all, *they had everything to live for*. There is something about the way certain rocks—not goats, rocks— stare out to sea in the sunlight even when there is no sea, no sky, no crystalline sea air but only a miasma—one third stench, one eighth vapor—that fills me with rude, even lewd, delight. And it pains me— that totally absorbed staring. Or rather, my prostration before the staring is inseparable from pain. Yes, the very condition of my observation becomes the occasion of my downfall. It is not that I crave the rock faces per se staring outward. I crave their absorption as a contemptuous repudiation. I crave not the rocks but the rocks' not needing me in the way I need them nor in any other way, since here they are looking out to sea, for all intents and purposes at sea, and here I am looking to them as if their very absorption was the sea's "inscrutable immensity." She looked as if "I crave not the rocks but the rocks' not needing. . ." was yet another desecration of the memory of meaning, recruitment of the always reliable paroxysms of syntax to the ultimate dismemberment of meaning as any self-respecting citizen had every right to know it. She replied: Although your dream is ostensibly to undergo a fruitful collaboration between my symptom, whatever that is, and your symptom, whatever that is, in actual fact you want to slough as fast as possible the viewpoint—the observations—your symptom has made possible, that is to say, impossible to ignore, in order to have done with them and by extension with the symptom and by surextension with any agonizing interconnection with my symptom and by sursurextension—in tandem—with me. For you the symptom—the craving—the hunger—the desire—the frothing at the mouth is the sum of occasional verses to which it has given vent and if only you can find a way to run out of such verses you thereby run out of the symptom and out of any craving to run with me.

Some goats approached: brother, sister, maiden aunt. She began to sweat. He murmured: Look at that rock face over there. She turned toward it: It has turned over, almost out of sight, and yet its rear remains conspicuous, dotted in fact with tiny hairs, though perhaps invisible to the unpracticed eye. Is that swerving away, from us, from the moment, from this goat trio, somehow fueled by the presence of the hair—the sense of potency lent by the hair—or is the swerving a sort of melancholy induced by the hairs conveniently construed as marring the perfect surface of immortality. As if to recapture her attention beleaguered by the goat group: It is unclear whether front and rear are linked in unity, present a unified front against the world or is the front ignorant of what the back is doing, being done to. And my excitement—my symptom—is it, after all, but an uncertain slavering before the inexpugnable conflation of front and back embodied in the smooth-tongued swerving beyond the swaying backside hairs. Is my craving in fact a marveling at the ease of unity between front and back, front easily subsuming all manifestations of back as well as of a million other facets infinitely more exiguous? Is my craving in fact a marveling before the ease—amounting to a kind of ruthlessness—with which the rock faces doughtily and proudly doughtily and proudly assimilate whatever grows on any of their other surfaces? Or am I slavering before the stark disjunction between front and backside, this facet and that, failed merging incarnated in a melancholy swerving toward flight from an infinity of facets with which communion is impossible? Is my symptom—my desire—my craving—at once born from and exacerbated by the failed unity/simultaneity of front, back, and an infinity of intermediate facets or rather by the boldly united front presented by front, back, and that infinity—presented by front to back and back to front? Or does the symptom—the craving—the hunger—my symptom—my craving—my hunger—reside in some shadowy substratum that has generated this question—the form of this question—as a camouflage? In short, there may be—there is—no answer to the question as I have posed it. The form of the question simply assures us the symptom is near. But: In their swerving do the rockfaces from pride or melancholy celebrate the hairy fissures they cannot see or is the swerving simply or not so simply affiliated with other meanings—meaning I cannot begin to dream of?

Rising—he realized suddenly she had been sitting—she announced that she intended to take the several little ones on a trip, away from the unhealthiness of rocks and goats, rocks merely standing in for whatever goats were on convalescent leave. Unaccountable burst of delight knowing she and the little ones would be gone at last and he with the opportunity to explore at length all he had been recounting. For what he had been telling her was new also to him, outlining what at present was only a prospective craving. There was still some unfinished business to attend to, in fact, all truck with the rocks was, tautologically, unfinished business. Or were his bowels desecrating the memory of meaning once more.

Once she and the little ones, who had been playing a little way off, were gone and as I made my way toward them—the rock faces—after a less than hearty breakfast [appetites, in my case, being mutually exclusive] it became unclear to me [always a sign that I was still very much alive, when something became and *a fortiori* had the goodness to remain unclear] whether my unfinished business was mild habituation to the rocks among the rocks or splintering collision with their surfaces, hairy or not. I sat myself down by the water and found myself noting less rocks than passersby. These insignificant others made it a point to pass by the rocks with their intricacy of little hairs veining surfaces and clogging interstices every chance they got. But I could tell from their looks that for these the rocks were a given *en bloc*, a datum never to be brooded through interpretation because incapable of fascination through generation of minute differences. He was eager for these to be gone, their presence saddened. Once again he noted that although certain smooth, even glabrous, faces had fissures baldly clogged with dark coarse bristles these did not prevent them from adopting the air, highly ethereal, of seaward-facing porpoises. Did this mean they were able to advance in the direction of their real purpose without being in any way stymied by what the cloggedness, the sprawling daring of the dark bristles, coarse and damp, evoked of a countervailing stance appropriate to—earmarked for—beings so marred—something on the order of a sludgelike rootedness in unformed anticipatory lust? And if they were in fact advancing was it in full knowledge of the downward-pulling clogged fissures or in total unawareness? Or did they somehow manage to embrace these backward-looking surfaces smeared with mossy sludge as in no way incompatible with advance? Were they in no way stymied, then, by what the fissures said or threatened at some point to say but rather immeasurably enriched by what they succeeded in categorizing as but another facet of their multeity and only a possible facet at that? And did this blithe acceptance of a gross—the grossest—physical fact enhance their strength?

And there were other rocks, not necessarily clogged but lightly stroked with bristles and seeming sad. What made for the sadness of the rocks? The mere presence of the bristles or the failure somehow to unite the smooth flawless delicacy of their fronts and the lumpish clogging of their nonfronts into some single statement worthy of a whole being? Of course their sadness might have nothing to do with the grossness of physical fact. Only this he did not wish to believe. [For some of their imbecile congeners unity had to come easy especially when their posteriors looked far more expressive than their fronts.] He could feel himself progressing toward an axiom to govern the wide range of his confusion and its inexorably maddening inducement of interpretation: To wit, clogged fissures, vast rents clogged with even vaster flayings of coarse matted hair—whether seen and appropriated by their hosts, just seen, or unseen—were somehow constitutive of a brash being in stone—

9

a model fearlessness in the face of life's improprieties. Yet here were some of the streaked and flayed streaked with melancholy. And he could not help imagining that the melancholy was directed at—had been provoked by—the minute hairs pullulating among downward-pulling rearward-looking faces. Sitting and trying to make sense of the rocks he *found himself* giving way to despair until—rather, all the more forcibly when—he reminded that self there was no conceiving it, or rather its fragments, apart from a conceiving of the mineral world and its mysteries, apart from a prostration before its contradictions that were contradictions, however, only when the beam of his consciousness was trained upon it, which contradictions became in turn the target of his desire or rather and more accurately the only way into that desire. Or was he again—and after all he had been told— desecrating the memory of meaning as every good citizen has a right to preserve it.

Now he came across some rocks that fell short, far short, of perfection. Yet his craving—his desire—his hunger—did not decrease: on the contrary intensified, or rather something intensified that ended up distracting him from what his desire was doing. All this as he went about striving to understand what demon of perversity could entice this particular target—this particular rock face—into withholding perfection. And what was the secret superfetatory strength of this target enabling it to survive perfection's absence after having manufactured said absence. On such themes he meditated as the sun set and he realized he was awaiting her return—expecting that at any moment she and the little ones would catch him in the act—far more naked than the forms he was contemplating—of abstention.

He cried out:

ABSTENTION

but he was terrified of living up to the demands of any rubric or of being able to contrapose to the rubric as an element of decor—textual, conversational—a body of observations relating to the rubric and sufficiently substantive to justify such an indulgence, that is to say, swamp and obliterate the rubric in its hiding place. The minute he had a heading he was the enervated prisoner of that heading, sagitally charting his course for the next few milliseconds. He was preparing himself, as they approached, to tell all, regarding his abstention from act. Then he realized he did not have to tell all: They were not his confessor. He did not want a confessor in the story—yet—and so he was in no manner obliged to surrender to the telling of his abstaining from the definitive act that must seal his connection to the rock faces forever. He knew in advance of the telling that telling of abstention would be—must be—a far more difficult telling than that assigned to adits and exits to and from the definitive act. For there is a certain boldness that rubs off on the telling from the acts themselves when the telling is a telling of one's acts, however unspeakable. Whereas abstention from act belongs to no country yet is reprehensible in all. There was no need to speak yet of abstention. Nor might there ever be. As they approached—they were approaching still, coming up one cliff, then down another, in quest of the smooth plateau that separated them from him and him from them— in the violent sunlight a few of the forms seemed to be applauding, winking, at his strenuous efforts to confront whatever demons were latent in their facets. The applause was completely disorienting even if the applause was most definitely not a thing replete unto itself, with beginning, middle, intermission, and end, but rather a ticlike and inter- mittent goad to what could only be interpreted as investigation, deeper and deeper and further and further along the lines of whatever at present merited investigation enjoining and inseparable from a closing himself off from her, more and more, from the little ones, her symptom, their symptoms, The applause clearly decreed that investigation was incompatible with what he had heard called *home life*. If he was to be a model for the little ones, how could he go about prostrating himself before the rock faces even if it was a heuristic prostration. Although strictly speaking it would not be prostration for he knew how to dissimulate: When struck dumb by the sinuous contour of one rock he immediately turned in the opposite direction so as to give the impres- sion not of focused craving but of a quaquaversal parrying of blows.

Returned at last she looked mournful, to say the least, though she was keeping up a brave front for the sake of the little ones, growing *bigger and brighter* with each passing day. I know where you've been, said she. His smile at the children was immediately understood by both to mean, Where. With the goats: You pay them for your pleasure. He turned from her to the rocks that before his very eyes seemed to be growing. He let them. One particularly stippled and vibrant surface began to overwhelm him, growing tremulousness fast rendering him unfit for any further contact with her, with the little ones. My little ones, he said. He turned to her then back to the rock in question and from that rock to the sky, as if turning to the sky was equivalent to a turning back to her and that life of which conjointly they had managed to make a shambles. All the time he had his eye on the sky and its flaws of glassy rack he was hoping that when he rested his eyes once again on the rock in question it would no longer be the rock in question, simply indistinguishable from its brethren—in short, and for all practical purposes, gone and its being gone and having quit the scene undoubtedly for good equivalent to his annulled susceptibility to prostration before its likes—the likes of its imperial obliviousness to his—which annulment must qualify as a being rendered suddenly fit for contact with the little ones and with their mother. You paid them, didn't you, she continued. You paid the goats. He waited a long time before adding, The goats. I know, I know, she parried, squeamish, as if out of the blue I had chosen to bring up something untoward and unspeakable which something needlessly brought up might very well end up existing. She could speak of the goats a thousand times a day: it was simply not the same thing. For her speaking of the goats was a warding off of the goats, a moving testimony to her stalwart refusal to conceive of my conceiving of—much less desiring—the goats or that the goats might ever exist outside her whimsical and intermittent resurrection of their nonbeing twenty, thirty, forty, ninety times a day. She named them to hold them at bay, somewhere on the marshy margins of being. The more she dwelt on his relation to the goats the more it took on the character of an internal construction. But a word from me, a word spewed mindlessly, a word like, Nanny, or Billy, redressed the balance in favor of an external goad prefiguring her catalysis.

As the little ones wished to play and as both she and I needed some respite from this joust of symptoms, we succeeded in fumbling toward a little playground overlooking a bight removed from the sea. As they made their way ahead I pitied them struggling alone in the growing twilight. For for a split second I forgot I was there, to protect them, at the very least to interpose my churlish bulk should danger threaten. Here, on the highway leading to the playground, I was reminded the world is a loathsome place. Yet as we proceeded I loathed equally every sign from her, of which there was suddenly an overabundance, that I was needed, more than needed, obliged and expected to grab whatever muniments would entitle them to a place in the sun. We were bound into duration. The children—the little ones—took to the playground quickly enough, screamed to hear themselves scream. There were other families, real ones, I mean, where the mothers and fathers liked, it was clear, being indentured into brute duration, their tinny voices echoing as in the kitchen of eternity while dutifully they discussed that evening's dinner and whose underwear needed most scouring or scalding in the next day's wash. They were reassured by their own sounds. I could only dream of freeing myself so that the mystery of the rock faces would reveal itself at last.

I looked around. At first the objects made me sick, mere props, decorative applied art. But then one or two things emerged that were indisputable by-products of exertions proper to this time and place. Two squashed cans of soda pop were propped up on the bench beside me. I smiled at the little ones trying to sit up unaided on the bench beside the sandbox. But I could not point out to her, could not bear partaking with her, of this spectacle even if at moments it felt as if I was sorely tempted. For saying what I saw could only bind me more forcibly to—in—duration and force back to zero the sum of grievances I was carefully conserving in the silence vital to their germination. I moved away as I heard her attempt to go on about how the older ones were mimicking the littler ones, testing their outcries over varying distances. She was trying to lure me into behaving like the others. I got up and went in search of a receptacle for the two squashed cans. For they had suddenly outlived their uselessness, so to speak. They no longer embodied the desperate and necessary exertions that had formed them and were now just like any other scraps of decor. Inscribed in duration's shadow, the other men and women, mothers and fathers, husbands and wives, still seemed particularly pleased to be making their small contribution—through vociferous parentage, through preoccupation with dinner and the smelly wash—to eternity's upkeep. They were positively exhilarated by their impersonation of *what everybody else must be like.*

I wanted to have done, be gone, flee, but how flee with a horde of goats suddenly advancing on the monkey bars. Here they were, scavenging in a leisurely way and ogling—positively ogling—her—our—offspring. Oddly enough, caught in the sunburst of the dying day she said nothing, only smiled, warmly, appreciatively. Docile, absorbed, almost inanimate she was suddenly possessed of a potent fragility. I did not know how to react to this failure to respond in her usual way. Though why call it failure, this translucent slab of calm salvaged from the quarry of her usually exorbitant erithism in the face of every—the merest possibility of—goat event. As the troop wandered off and she let them go without a word, without a look, without meaningful looks in my direction, I could not take my eyes away from the back of her head, the mass of uncoiled hair, as the embodiment of suddenly potent fragility. Deciding not to comment, not to remind her of what goats normally signified, though why should I want to remind her, I became her caretaker, caretaker of her consciousness, of her lapse from consciousness, lapse to living silently, serenely, to the side or behind her usual—her traditional—self.

It was she who asked if we could move on now, her moving on an embodied innocence. There was beauty in her having forgotten the goats in relation to me due to absorption in an elsewhere impossible to pinpoint. What was keeping her from her usual stratagems for making sure I was or was not acting in conformity with the dictates of her symptom? This receding troop of goats moved me deeply, born as they were from a collision with her unseeing. Through her involuntarily respectful unseeing the goats were coming alive. They were coming alive as they traversed layer upon layer of the ever-widening density of that unseeing seeing, unhearing hearing, with which they had to contend. It was as if the goats were at last being disclosed to me. The goats were being presented according to the specifications of her failure to grasp them. Forced to traverse ever-widening layers of this density of her being elsewhere they came more alive. Her inadvertent resistance, her indifference, to their now canonical virulence, to questioning the phenomenon that was the trooping goats on their deepest level, created it—the phenomenon—at long last. Her unseeing seeing, her being focused elsewhere and not on their capacity to lure me away, her resistance to being made anxious, did away with all of mine, leaving me free to contemplate. Perhaps it was because of this incident, or absence of incident, that in the middle of the night, the night following that day, I underwent a solemn and uncontrollable hunger for her. At the same time I was disappointed by the very intensity of this craving. For I was now used, compliments of the rocks, to the virulence of overweening desire being constrained to traverse a defile of narrowly increasing intensities. She gave herself to me, all the time murmuring it was the goats I wanted, always the goats, the goats I was penetrating, front, back, below.

I returned to the rocks, unable to decide whether or not to put myself into that particular relation or absence of same to which I had become somewhat inured. After the visit to the playground, with her and the little ones, it was more difficult. Or rather, it was more difficult after having seen her and the little ones alone and defenseless, without a protector, posthumously, as it were, having forgotten to insinuate myself into the tableau. But was it in fact more difficult now to reestablish my relation to the rocks and if more difficult because of the playground visit or the failure to insinuate myself as protector within the confines of their blighted tableau? Maybe this is all hogwash and I am simply trying to turn the playground incident into an incident, that is to say, into some kind of pivotal avatar of meaning as the scholiasts know and love to chew it up, bones and all. Maybe it seemed more difficult only because the playground incident—the celebrated playground sequence—was so disorienting it quite destabilized my relation to the memory of how difficult things had in fact been. Someone was now standing to the side of the shoulder of one of the rock faces that usually caught my attention. At first I took him for another rock or wanted to. But as I moved away he moved with me. As I began walking faster and faster, conscious once again of the caltrops to which my concern for the contour of the landscape was exposing me, I remembered the little ones, so playful in and out of the sun's rays, and found myself feeling most judged by them. For in my pursuit of the rocks I was abandoning them, proclaiming a scandalous obsession with undulating fissures at the very moment when their very different nakedness urged an attentiveness, a fatherly calm, my comings and goings clearly could not vouchsafe.

Soon I was out of harm's way, if, that is, the mover had meant me any harm. I had moved too fast, I was incomprehensible to myself, no more than what it—the mover—had understood me to be based on my response to the signs it had given. Into what had it transformed me, my pursuer's pursuit. In my sweaty flabby panic—I remembered the rocks, the crowd of rocks, recoiling; they recoiled now—I suddenly incarnated all I loathed but the incarnation brought me no closer to a sense of myself. Its pursuit was the form of my disintegration. I thought back over the terrain of pursuit, if that was what it had been. But I could not appropriate it, annex it. Shamefully formless, either intrinsically or in the way I recuperated it, pursuit overcame me first at every tourney. I checked to see if I had lost anything: I had the distinct impression of having lost something, a something that might be everything. Now alone it seemed my relation to the rock faces would never end and that being endless it cried out for—was made to the measure of—some confessor. Someone to appropriate what promised to be a long line of dire encounters disguised as ungainly pursuits. I moved a small distance away but still I could not surmount the sense of having lost something that might be everything. I hadn't the faintest idea what it was except that something surely had changed hands in the moment when I came undone at the sight of the other advancing. All I knew was that the more precious the object the more irrevocable must be the loss. In the damp glow of evening—it was as if I had commandeered the curdling grey of the heavenly burial grounds to train its arclight on the site of prior confusions—I could not quite discern the where and what of that site. Still I walked around what I took to be a plausible approximation of the site. For something was gone, lost forever, and when there is loss there is a site of loss. I raged against myself, so preoccupied with a quick getaway I hadn't been aware something was gone. I began to moan, as she might have done, as I had on many occasions seen her do, when for example one of the little ones stayed out long after nightfall or insisted on hitting its head repeatedly against a beech tree's inscriptions. Over, no retrieving the essential. At that moment one of the older little ones passed me by, or simply passed by. I wondered if he could see I had lost something. He leaped across a little pool with a gauging intrepidity that told me he hadn't seen me. The fear inside the intrepidity was presented as clearly as an X-ray. When finally he did see me he looked anxious for we were meeting out of context, context meaning the hovel in which he had been born and raised. It was up to me to enable us both to survive this absence—no, shift—in context. But how consecrate myself to such a project when I had just lost something vital to the execution of any project. Up to me. All eyes—his two—upon me. Up to me to prove I recognized, that is to say, loved him and that this feeling was not a mere excrescence of habit wanly damply germinated elsewhere and intractable to transplantation to an absence of—to a shift in—context. I felt mercilessly under his surveillance for as the more helpless, less inventive, less officially entrenched in the ways of being, he had a right to sit back and watch, that is, recoil in judgment. I could actively strive either to create a fresh context or thrash and gurgle toward annihilation of all hope for context.

And as was frequently the case, it seemed that rehabilitation with respect to the rocks was contingent on resolution of the challenge now confronting me. I had the unseasonable delusion—a mere somersault of pseudo-meaning synthesized for the delectation of those who might pay no heed to my story without such sops?—that if only the ratchet wheel of my craving could collide with and catch on some pawl-like incontrovertibly real object—distillation, as it were, of all others—with subsequent inevitable enhancement of a sense of being to the point of reconstitution from my own ashes, then I would no longer need to seek obliteration among the rocks and all would be well. I harbored the delusion that before slavish slimy descent into the kingdom of the rocks' hair-clogged fissures if only I could abut on some object or incident served up as object—some unforeseen collision capable of hoisting my self-esteem, that is, of reconstructing my identity from scratch and thereby hallucinating my sodality with the accursed human race in contradistinction to the race of venated minerals—then I would be spared once and for all the inevitable pacing, back and forth and up and down and away, sometimes even far away, in anticipation of the moment desolate and therefore supremely appropriate—but from whose perspective?—for entry into that wretched realm. The presence of the little one out of his usual context, that singlehandedly subserved by her, his mother, seemed to offer just the restorative collision I was looking for. I took his hand out of his mouth, brushed back his hair, announced to the rocks the nature of our relation. At the same time I felt it was all an act: I had no right to be stroking his pink little face: He who prostrates himself before the rock faces is not adequate to the creation of new contexts. I told him he must not judge me too harshly, I was not as grotesque as rumor might have it, and that whatever happened he was to try to go on loving me as best he could. When he was gone how far away it now seemed, pursuit by that thing—that other—and the momentary desire for a confessor that it bred. How far away it seemed, the last epsiode of prostration before the rock faces, here and there clogged and striated. So far away that I could have only contempt for my desire and for my panic in the face of that desire and even for the unmoving forms that had inspired it, to say nothing of the marginal thing that had pursued in the marginal hope of making me pay dearly for it. I could only chortle at that far-off terrorized belief in an incapacity to survive without aid of a confessor. In my sudden rage, yes, rage, over the faint flinty repulsiveness of all things I could not understand the mewling of such a belief. Even if I already sensed that such astonished outraged estrangement often masking handseled a relapse of the very same thralldom. The first stage is always exasperated incomprehension at the floundering of some one among an infinity of repudiated selves.

As I walked toward the gulls perched along the line of bollards planted absurdly upright in all that waste of trash-colored sand I underwent their staggered flight at my approach as the inevitable and organic prolongation of my own movement—always away from all former selves—I underwent their flight away from my approach well before it made itself known [for some of these creatures were mighty slow in complying with the demands of a petty atavism] and in fact I underwent their movement as more my movement than my own. For movement of the gulls was a movement away and what had my movements always been but a poor poor relation of same. I looked back, the little one a mere pinpoint among the juttings and carvings. But he was calling to me, running toward me, and when he reached me asked that I escort him back to the hovel that was home, sweet home. Afraid, he said. Of what, I asked. Goats in the rocks and rocks in the goats, he answered, but it was more like a demand. Goats in the rocks and rocks in the goats, he shivered. The shiver announced that he had developed a symptom in response to hers, in respone to mine. This was his contribution to the family fund. This newfound fear of making his way along the wellworn paths alone was all I needed to resuscitate a craving for return to the rocks and to the clogged fissures that were their mutilated heart.

His newfound symptom and the sense that I was in some way responsible was all I needed of unpleasantness as goad and foothold toward the by now old inebriating prostration. This—a little one's cry from the heart targeted directly at the heart of my own criminal negligence—was all I needed to propel me back into the morass. My soul or whatever could be claimed as the site of criminal negligence contracted: I and I alone was responsible for the little one's budding misery, his esemplasticizing response to misery through symptom-making. As I was leaving the outskirts of the hovel—though the hovel was strictly and even not so strictly speaking all outskirts—she stopped me, eyeing with rage and contempt the incontrovertible source of the little one's phobia, or rather, what was far worse, predisposition to phobia. I contracted again but this time contraction was instantaneously transformed into a joyous expansion: I was defective and ineluctably the cause of another's budding defect. I was a walking morass—for wasn't that the message of the raging contempt, the shadowy eyeing as I attempted to make my escape—and worthy only of shameful prostration before the shadowy forms overlooking the sea. I was linked to a judge—a hanging judge—she—and her condemnation made my pursuit of these forms urgent and at the same time safe for now I would be pursuing them in the tutelary shadow of her judgment—something to return to—a foothold beyond the rocks themselves among which I was always afraid of drowning.

Armed only and exorbitantly

But no matter how enormous his symptom—I could hear him weeping within the hut as the others fought for scraps—he could not bear to stay alone in my bed—his bed—my bed, not even with all the other little ones surrounding me—him: The goats, the rocks, the goats, were invading. But I did not want to take matters to a stranger—a confessor. Even though—precisely because—I was having so many thoughts that were confessor fodder. As much as I wanted to get rid of them I wanted to hold on to all they embodied of desire, craving, hunger—desire, craving, hunger foiled in its quest for a target out there and taking consolation amid the intricate pathways of a telling almost told. Why not hold on to these thoughts rather than dump them down the nearest annihilatory chute.

Armed only and exorbitantly

Yet I had so much to tell another, some other, some certified other, about these fissures made not to be enjoyed but rather described. Withheld from the circumstances proper to description these thoughts became a pathway to freedom or a far more potent substitute for freedom. Or rather, I had now to go about seeing whether withheld these thoughts . . . about rocks and their fissures and the tiny hairs clogging fissurely respiration could be transformed into something better than everything they were about, than themselves, than thought itself. More and more tailored to a confessor's impatience more and more I was intent on withholding them. Hurrying off I decried a flock of goats and for a split second it seemed she had right on her side: If I concentrated I might be able to interest myself in their shape, their expression, their shamelessness. I went on hurrying but couldn't be sure if it was away from her or from the rocks. These were after all the twin foci whence every pinpoint of my being recoiled according to the following formula: I was the locus of all twinges the sum of whose distances from these twin foci was always the same cipher: despair plus selfloathing divided by flight time—elliptic magisterium of my nonbeing. Already I was knowing this confessor only too well—as one for whom the thought-inducing moments of prostration would come to serve as the warmed-over meat of professional enrichment. I would end up furnishing instance after instance of self-diminishing prostration so that his professional vehicle might remain afloat. I saw him already entering the harbor of recertification.

I sensed her in back of me. I needed something to oppose to her encroachment, armed only and exorbitantly with

The little one's symptom had set her off. I knew her: The last straw. Yet did I really need the confessor to oppose to her ghastly growing encroachment? Wasn't it rather the story that needed him— it—or rather his encroachment—as a meaning—as a potential repository of meaning—to be opposed to hers—no longer merely potential. Meaning is a convenience that the story, like an invalid emboldened by bedsores, feels entitled to. Meaning is an extemporized roadblock against story twists and turns gone paroxysmal.

Whether or not she was advancing there was little more to be extracted from the rocks—with or without the shadow of her condemning pursuit—without the addition of a confessor. I felt myself running out of meaning. What's more I could see her always getting closer, her hair pulled back from a knotted forehead, giving to her bearing a purity of indomitableness in the face of circumstance. She cried out: Come back. I said, without any effort to make my voice carry, that I wasn't done with the rocks. She shook her head, presumably at my obstinacy, and did two things: muttered, The goats, the goats, and made a mechanical gesture to embody the obstinacy. I knew my cue, no matter if it didn't come from her: Upon this gesture I promptly leaped as for dear life for the gesture's insistence suggested an infinite strength, rootedness, that naturally appealed to one of my ilk not for the purpose of manly emulation but as something impregnable and surefooted against which spinelessly to butt in ridiculing disdain. Discovery of this gesture as a pretext for humorous incursion was an occasion for the most riotous celebration until I found myself wondering whether or not she was intending to give way to hot tears. And while I was still deciding whether or not to commit the colossal imprudence of showing compassion she said, invalidating my discovery in one swoop, You'll never leave me for the rocks. I felt she was about to add: And for the clefts in the rocks. And as much as I wanted or thought I wanted to answer I could say nothing. And before I could take stock of the effect of this saying nothing—But what effect could a creature such as I have on her, much less on little ones? I dared her to try to suggest an impact on their development or perverse refractoriness to same that would not be outrageously—inconceivably—disproportionate to my carefully planned marginality in that domain—before I could take stock she added: You don't realize the effect you have—on them, on me—running off every chance you get—to the rocks. I mean, the goats. The goat faces.

I could not answer. She was tactlessly obstructing my freedom to entertain a possibility. Even if I had no intention of abandoning myself to the rocks why should that future be proscribed. I refused to be so shorn. So I said nothing and she wept. I wanted to move on, into the realm of the rocks—even the confessor's would do, anywhere but here. But on I sat, stroking her forearm as if it was the source and center of her pain. Skirting the rocks as I escorted her home—second escort detail in the course of a mere few hours—we came upon a mutual acquaintance, a farmer, sucking on the tits, or is it at the tits, of not one goat but three. Observing him completely given up to this exertion I could not but feel a certain ecstasy. Not for his doings *per se* but because they put me in the clear, not just for now but for all time. If the goats were jealous of each other our friend the farmer did not seem to care in the least. Yet his licking was more than a mere self-satisfied licking. The licking, the manner in which he licked, something, seemed to imply that this simultaneous licking of tits belonging to three differ-ent goats was a solution, sublimely elegant—in the mathematical sense—to a problem that was no longer simply just their problem but the problem with which we all begin and end.

And on a less exalted level he was showing that he among so many also-rans had been able—as I, for example, hadn't—though suddenly it appeared I had recruited the rocks or they had recruited me for just such a purpose—to erect an act rectifying all prior acts marred by him or by anybody even dimly connected with him for that matter. Licking and sucking he had managed to stumble on a state of affairs proving he was equally withdrawn from and remiss with regard to everyone, without preference, including his three goats. I couldn't be-lieve there were only three goats: it seemed his blandishments were confined to an infinity at the very least. Curious about her reaction, I eyed her from the side. Here, after all, were her worst fears being realized. I was waiting for her to embrace me, gratefully. Our hovel came into view. He, the eldest little one, was gesticulating madly, seemed to be shrieking. Obviously he could no longer bear to be alone: with the goats and the rocks and the rocks in the goats and the goats in the rocks. She said nothing, kept walking, but I knew she would have to end up embracing me. For all the toxins engendered by my craving for the goats had clearly been drawn off into the bloodstream of Farmer von Scheiss. In fact so relieved—so grateful—did I expect her to be, for the fact that I was not he, von Farmer Scheiss, nothing like him in fact, just sucking away there, that I was already promising myself—a bit truculently, I have to admit—a little public fit commemorating the fact that he—and not I—had been permitted this indulgence. I was waiting for her, as she turned away presumably searching for the sparkle over the sea, to abase herself to the level of a plea that I never take it into my head to do what Farmer von Scheiss had taken it into his mouth to do. I was awaiting the inevitable. We had already left the good farmer far behind, still being given suck, though the goats were pretending to kick him away.

Not only did the sight of Scheiss and his goats—still before my eyes though far far behind—furnish a welcome distraction from the failures and terrors of domestic intimacy—she had to be too much in shock to be able to think of berating me for my multitudinous defects— it also handseled, like the sediment falling to the bottom of a beaker, an identity. I was: for I was what Scheiss was not; what Scheiss, lost among his acts, could never be. Having staked a claim to what I could never expropriate now he had gotten there first and last he left me free to ride roughshod over other possibilities. He had realized something I need no longer strive toward, not that I had ever noticed myself striving toward it or even away from it. Only the shadow of Scheiss sucking at the three grandiose tits was a retrospective glow over the past—my past—that disclosed all the holes, the lacks, the bland velleities. His shadow transformed that past into the ashes of a hopeless striving toward the very state of affairs he had managed to call his own. So I was envying and resenting Scheiss because hadn't he come upon a way of being in the world that was his very own? which was more than I could say for myself, and to one without a way every way looks good. And at the same time I disdained his way and sighed with relief that it was not *my* very own since when all was said and done it was just one more way among an infinity of ways, all inhearsed in finitude and doomed to disintegration.

She surprised me. There was no gratitude, no simpering relief, when she said, Are you going to live with us and be a real father to the little ones and a real husband to little me at last. And stop beating me to death. I was not sure in what sense I was supposed to be beating her to death. But I knew if I asked she would shrug with exasperation. It was clear the doings—the very existence—of Farmer Scheiss von was my proof, yet another proof of my dire anomalousness. Though he had been her neighbor too it was I who was singlehandedly responsible for consigning her to a world of marginalia—first, the rocks, now Farmer von der Schiss. Instead of thanking me for being oh so very much unlike the reprehensible Farmer Scheissendorf and his band of merry macaques, she was reproaching me for having somehow managed to insinuate him into her line of vision and especially at the very moment when her one thought was to get home, prepare dinner, contend with the little ones' symptoms, old and new. So Farmer Scheiss had turned out to be not a merry distraction but rather one more in a lineage of indignitaries introduced by me—one more straw to break the camel's backside. Here I was come this vast distance whence the good farmer had already receded to a mere pinpoint of shadow basely defrauded in my expectation that he and his trio would manage to create a celebratory space in which my instantaneous righteousness—necessarily a contrasting righteousness—the puny righteousness of contradistinction—would entitle me to exculpated prostration before the fur-lined rocks. I had expected her to be so appalled by the image of a man and three goats as to emerge almost grateful for my relatively harmless philandering among the faces. But she was not grateful. She continued to eye me warily. I had been so sure of that gratefulness that I had anticipated not only a space celebratory of my non-Scheissian righteousness [whence to catapult myself in times of need back to the lair] but within that edifice of air a little freehold to be specifically set aside for those occasional outbreaks of petulance to which, piously abstaining from all gambols even remotely resembling those of the von Scheissian variety, I was serenely entitled, and that were serenely entitled in turn to engender little voyages, among the rocks. Arriving home directly she put the little ones to bed and came to me, sadly. The eldest would not stay in the other room. He insisted on remaining with us, or rather, between us. He finally fell asleep at our feet. Armed only and exorbitantly with her suspicions she pushed me away, having decided that if Father von Scheiss had seen fit to indulge in such practices then clearly I could not be too far behind. She felt obliged to point out that my nails were not only chewed down to the bone but overlong, my hair was also too long, my armpits were rancid with sweat, my teeth caked with a bister of regret for what only I could be held accountable. And I, the traditionally oversuspected, took all this with a good—the best—grace, that is to say, amid a clatter of pots and pans and the chatter of little ones awakening I cursed her cursing me and left half-accoutred for my regular ramble among the rocks.

Armed only and exorbitantly

I stormed out pursued by her ululations. Something about the success of her sister's husband, which quickly became something about my inveterate refusal to rejoice in the well-earned success of others. Didn't I know their success plausibilized my own? This conception— rather, this construction—fascinated me. Not only the ferny grasslands but the rocks themselves seemed to part as I propelled myself down the steeps toward perdition. My immediate concern was now for the rocks and for the rocks alone: There was nothing between her and me. I was living, so I now told myself, for the rocks alone, or rather, only for rectification of my image in their eyes. For parting so smoothly toward the grasses and rocks I tried to make my retreating buttocks signify the purest gratitude untinctured by the sneering bravado typical of one who through no skill of his own has effected a fast getaway. At the same time I tried to regulate the language of these buttocks, immediately replaying their gyrations with the eye of the rocks and grasses, to ensure that I whatever I had given in the way of thanks was adequate to the situation and did not eternally brand me as one who at the meanest civility is given to unwholesome prostration before essentially torpid and unresponding forms. I arrived before the sea in one piece. I assumed my descent had been successful for I could distinguish no rearward hissing among the stubbly wallows, no rocky backlash. Arriving where the most interestingly fissured forms were huddled I was struck—though not quite dumb—with admiration for a night so calm and so exquisitely starless. In fact, I feared I was going to be punished for what now appeared to be the flamboyant ease of my trek even if such ease was a well-earned reward for all the turmoil endured at the hovel. So, depending on whether I underwent the descent as the complementary and compensatory descending arm of the curve of my squabble at the hovel, in which case the ease with which it had been accomplished could be taken—and rightly—as a reward well-earned and long overdue, or as the ascending arm of a curve both new and unknown, in which case its emblematic ease would surely encounter a nemesis-laden complement some time in the near future—depending on whether I underwent descent as one or the other I was alternately relieved or apprehensive.

Alone among the rocks at last: There was a relief in having abjured them all for ever and ever. Which is not to say I did not preserve some charming memories. Only it had taken a total severance from their breeding ground to enshrine them. I remembered, as the moon rose or set or the stars exploded one by one or two by two, the littlest little one undergoing his cycle of excitations the moment she glanced its way and persisting long after she had turned, ogling no more, now preoccupied, for example, with the imminently dire fate of the eldest little one: afraid to stay alone, to eat alone, to shit and piss alone.

Armed only and exorbitantly as only women can be

Here I was alone at last with the rocks yet able to think only of a confessor, some thing or someone to fling my uttered history right back in my face with that inflection of slander endemic to even the most faithful echo.

Armed only and exorbitantly with her raging suspicions, with the pigheaded insistence of her symptom that mine must be its sole cause and purest effect, she was waiting until I was momentarily lost to sight. A kitchen knife sticking out of her satchel she fixed her eyes always only on the few paces directly ahead of her, whenever, that is, there were a few paces to be had amid all that clutter of blackly buoyant vegetation. Catching sight of me once again she immediately noted the shabbiness of the seat of my pants. No wonder I had managed never to succeed at anything. It was clear she no longer loathed me simply for the symptom loaned me by her own and to which it was incumbent, given the furor of her perseverations, I be at all times delivered up. She loathed every aspect of my being. Yet how was she going to reconcile her revulsion with the purported fascination I exerted over the goat community. Running along the shore I cursed the rocks as if divested of my craving I could have expected all to be well. If only I hadn't succumbed to the supremely infantile luxury of being exactly what I was—if only I had managed—what could have been simpler?—to be another, he, she, or it sketched by her exasperation. She was now out of sight. No longer seeing her armed only and exorbitantly I strode back and forth before a particularly conspicuous entry into the nether paradise of the rocks. I wanted her to witness me actively abstaining from the solicitations of one among an infinity of fascinating outcroppings. I wanted her to witness me actively abstaining even if I myself did not know from what precisely, whether from rocks or from goats or from rocks inside goats or goats inside rocks. I anticipated her coming upon me from various angles and always discovering me free of taint—innocent—innocent—yet innocent in terms of whose symptom, hers, mine, or the little one's? Not that I cared—care—but the story, our story, waiting in the wings, arriving on the wings of her armedness—only but exorbitantly—cares, wants to know, needs to mean. If I was innocent of all relation to the goats where was the meaning—the percentage—in that? Innocence of that sort meant less than nothing: Why shouldn't I abstain from goats since I neither loved nor loathed them? But so strong was the impact of another's—her—interpreting consciousness or rather my consciousness of that encroaching interpreting consciousness that the mere prospect of her coming upon me to discover all her worst fears unfounded was more than enough to transform my goat-related innocence into something substantive—something on which to found a brave new world of ever-lasting identity.

Could I reconstitute our relation based on this sustenance to be derived from her misinterpretation of my postures? In any event, as she advanced I was transformed in my own eyes seeing myself with hers but once she moved off into shadow I lost track of an aura of innocence that in the face of the inevitable next onslaught of prostration before a particularly seductive slant of slab could only be momentary. As I went on walking before this or that very interesting outpouching brandishing all the features that made for an annihilating flash up the loins I told myself—over and over and over—that independent of any supercon-scious interpretations liberated by the briskness of her descent I was *innocent with respect to the rocks*. I was absolutely—isotropically—innocent. For I was abstaining from the rocks, no matter what flash they engendered up the loins. I was abstaining. But was my abstention

an authentic pathway to liberation or a mere puny defiance of somebody or some thing's illation that the rocks had become far too close for
comfort, which illation was equivalent to a fusion with the core of the
problem, my problem, which fusion could be made—was being made—
to stand in for my indissociability from my problem so that I might
conveniently go about my business elsewhere even in the total absence
of all business elsewhere—anywhere but in the vicinity of the rock faces
resisting my dread-laden efforts at fusion. It was clear I needed a
confessor if, that is, I was to go about my business elsewhere. I was now
hungering for a confessor almost as much as long before I had hungered
for the rock faces—someone or some thing to explicate my nonrelation
to the rocks, some thing so situated that at any given moment the sum
of his distances from me and any given rock, twin foci, would always be
the same. There was comfort in this—this constant that could be made
at a moment's notice to stand in for my own failed involvement in the
revels of the rocks and thanks to which—whose—which presence I
could at convenient intervals treat myself to a perfect furlough. No
doubt about it: I needed a confessor, one whose illations and computa-
tions concerning me and the rocks and the rocks and me could be
depended upon to lavishly subsidize an indeterminacy in behalf of
pursuit of my studies away from the only thing worth studying. It was as
if all of being was implying my only recourse was to a confessor. Or is
this last a trumped-up meaning produced unwillingly in ostensible
consternation and in fact delighted with itself? No point in pretending
any longer than I could live without this sportulary soul. But I tried not
to think of him, of it. For a confessor is an easy way out, leading
nowhere. It was up to me and me alone to enlighten the absence of a
relation to the rocks.

A leaf fell, from nowhere, to or from the rocks. And just when I
believed it dead to further movement there was a gratuitous, derisory,
posthumous somersault in a total absence of wind and as if tauntingly
on the margin of my apperception, already strained to breaking point,
suggesting an afterthought toward me on somebody or some thing's
part. So that when the next leaf fell I was prepared for a continuation,
that is, an intensification of what had become retrospectively a sign:
some continuation of plummet beyond and within the pavement of

undulation. For a second or two all of being seemed to share in the conspiratorial signifying of the rocks or the leaves or of some or all beings intermediate between rocks and leaves. Then just as suddenly everything conspired to go dead just like before. Only it wasn't as easy to accept as before. My nerves were so taut—and even if my nerves weren't so taut—I could no longer accept—*as before*—this absence of response—of intensification—as mere absence of response or intensification. Now absence of response was a unanimous and malignant attack on the frontiers of my being. As if all of being was implying my only recourse was to a confessor, that I must stop seeking sportulas among nature's dead and half-dead and go my own way to acceptable perdition. The rocks did not want me in the same way I reassured myself I wanted the rocks. If the rocky shore was the only conceivable domain for the playing out of my uncertainties then for the rocks themselves, the rocks themselves and their leafy fixtures, any connection with me in said domain was by most rigorous definition the flimsiest of interregnums preparatory—in the course of much prinking and preening—to far more serious revels elsewhere in which me and my uncertainties could not hope to have the smallest part.

I looked back, though standing still: The fall of the first leaf, or rather, its posthumous somersault, was already a point of demarcation in my life among the rocks and beyond, if I can speak of a life beyond what was already the farthest reach of my aspirations. Yet this point was already far distant. For I was already mounting toward new phenomena involving rocks and leaves on the very far side of which mounting the posthumous somersault ineptly cradled an infinity of contemned and discarded selves. There must come a time, I told myself, when I take myself severely to task for such a mode of nonbeing since it was precisely these selves and no others that constituting sponsored the vigor of ever-expanding contempt and hunger to discard directing, though hardly giving direction to, my life. I had to find a way to conflate them into an entity more potent than the craving that did them in. Just when it seemed I had exhausted all craving for the rocks a handsome young goat with a strong neck, sleek coat, shiny hair, large and bony head, firm jaws, deep chest, soft pliable skin, legs straight and sturdy, strong and straight pasterns, and rather large testicles, placed himself squarely in the path that led back to the hovel, the place where all the little ones—without exception—had been farrowed down in an ecstasy of unknowing regret. Before I could open my mouth, move, he began questioning me. Before I could make a few mild motions preparatory to reply he repeated the question, not from curiosity, so it seemed, but from a spasm instinct with martial duty, reflexive surrender to the precept that if he wished to suceed as goat, as—confessor, as both, as neither, he must miss nothing, must let nothing however trivial go by. And at the same time he seemed to be letting everything go by—not just me and my tics but the very flow of the rocks toward the sea and their posthumous somersault—like leaves! like leaves!—into the presumably briny depths or briny presumable depths so that it was no wonder he went on stamping and stamping: his way—a goat's—of both asking a question and demanding a repetition of the missed reply. Or maybe the second—the subsequent stampings were his sign that an initial intuition—that nothing was useful, nothing processable toward construction of a global concept fitted to, in other words, capable of obliterating, the target of his stampings—me—had been confirmed; that is, if the stamping and stamping and stamping wasn't a demand that I myself confirm the intuition. Perhaps confidently—blithely—exultantly—he was expecting mere repetition—in response to his stamping—to do the work of confirmation. Since few utterances can withstand the attenuation, might I even say the trituration, attendant on their repetition, especially a repetition grudgingly anticipated and condemned in advance.

So here he was, daring me to repeat whatever it was that had incited him to an initial riot of a curiosity impossibly constituted as frenetic demand for its repetition—repetition of the initially missed, just barely sensed and even then with distaste albeit a distaste pregnant with possibilities for future use. I could, then, be of use to him.

It was as if all of being was crying out that my only recourse

How ironic—how economical—that a goat—albeit a superb one—should see fit to install itself in the copiously dreaded and eagerly invoked too long vacant role of confessor for the excess of unspeakables induced by nonconnection to the rocks though not to be oozed out onto the rocks themselves. The craving to ooze the unspeakable was suddenly at least as intense as that for the rocks themselves. And now that our relation was established I was *literally* reeling from the effort to keep my head above the ooze. It did occur to me she might choose this moment to come upon us and mistake what she saw for a confirmation of her worst fears. Yet instead of her scrawny form rising up and out of the grey cloud that for so long had been hanging over the landscape was a whitish hillock, tinged with gold and shot through with that special inflection of sunlight mezzotinting the possibility of infinite happiness elsewhere. This fissure—like any fissure—in my routine [in other words, an earnest at last of real existence] expressed itself through routine light's transmogrification into a unique and wounding inflection. So I was ready to speak of them. It listened, or made as if to listen, occasionally wrinkling its bony nose or groin in sign of commiseration. But as I recounted my craving—my hunger—my desire—for the rocks, or rather, compulsive twistings and turnings before the most implausible points of entry that I hoped with the aid of his little beard he would be able to transform into craving—hunger—desire—but as I went on recounting I found myself getting more and more exasperated with his silence, whether or not a listening silence. It wasn't long before that silence, of listening or non-listening, less annihilating in fact as a non-listening, became a mighty virulence aimed directly at the pulpy craven heart of my desire—a remote and ponderous critique of desire. Yet what else could I possibly have expected? What could my desire as some thing directed toward uncertainty or my uncertainty as some thing directed toward desire or my desire once again as some pig directed toward its own bladder—what could any or all of these—the various stages of desire frozen into coexistence—have expected of a confessor? He—she—it—could easily see I was busy trying to convert my desire—my hunger—my craving—my symptom into something forever fresh, that is to say, multifariously scandalous to the point of near indigestibility, all in the name of perpetuating his function to the crack of doom even if he—she—it—he—had no wish, explicit or otherwise, for such perpetuation. Let's take it day by day, minute by minute, I could almost hear his dewlaps puling.

I wandered a short distance from Herr Goat. He stayed put. Who knows if he was sufficiently conscientious to keep me in his line of sight: I hadn't demanded references. He did look away as I advanced toward him, big with old news of my relation to him, to her, to the little ones. Though all of a sudden—so much of a change had this little relation with *my* confessor wrought in my being—I could not bear to think, much less return to, her.

Now, as I was approaching him and *a fortiori* the inevitability of speaking of her, of the little ones, *again*, I could only think back petulantly and envyingly and ungraciously on the *time before*—though what was the time before? where was it located? Somewhere, no doubt, in my movement away and my movement back—to him, the goat, Herr Goat—when I had suddenly found myself adapting far too easily to a rapture without bound and when the mere thought of an interruption of this rapture—this being held ecstatically in reserve—but for what?—for what?—through talk of her and of the little ones was met with eruptions of rage, disbelief. Yet here I was back again in his vicinity and didn't I know—from *long experience*—that being back in his vicinity meant nothing so much as being prepared to speak of her, even if speaking of her meant speaking of permanent abolition of the azure tints of ecstasy. Yet this appalling sense of a stark disjunction between before and after pivoted around some vanished seminal event seemed imported—transplanted—from some elsewhere into another, this, the elsewhere of my relation, the story of my relation, with the goat. But a certain scintillating core of the appalling sense had remained constant under transport and out of context—had in fact been enhanced, stretching and straining against the tight fit of present circumstances and was therefore resonating—scintillating—as itself and more than itself.

In the mean time she and the little ones were simply abolished by his bulk. In his protecting shadow there was no need to confess at the same time his shadowy substance was an inconstant reminder that confession was about to begin. And though I had been spared *for so long*, I was already adapting—adapted—to the necessity of *speaking to him once again* of her and of the hovel and of the little ones and of their budding symptoms and of how I had always managed to abandon them so mercilessly. Though as I spoke I was madly computing a way out of this resumed new—in fact very very old—life of telling, telling, telling: a life pivoted precariously around my laches. I was already striving to see my way clear to carving out a little niche of well-being from this edifice of reprobation, simultaneously addressing myself to the necessity of toning down any expectations of ecstasy, azure-tinted or otherwise. Ecstasy was slowly or quickly or moderately taking the form of whatever contrasts, high or low, I could manage to generate with what must surely prove—as long as it was a question of telling about her and the rocks and their unwavering incompatibility—a never-ending excruciation. Alas, it was no longer as it had been in that distended and infinitesimal interval between a going away and a coming back—to him and to the telling with which he expected to be upholstered—when, far away from her and the little ones and, better yet, a need to tell about her and the little ones, anything—yes, anything—was possible. No point waiting for rapture to redescend from the linden-scented azure. Now I had to train myself to exult over the precious minute or two that might, if I was lucky, fall to my lot between one bout of telling and the next. These were to be my eternity of pleasure even if *before*, when I was moving away from the goat but always in the comforting shadow of the goat, I would have deemed such a minute or two beneath notice. But now I had to get used to being far far far from that distant time of a moving away in the comforting shadow of a returning toward.

I spoke of how she weighed me down with her suspicions and of how I repelled her on every front. He looked bored, or rather, self-congratulatorily forbearing. He went on looking bored. After urinating on his beard he turned toward the sea, giving himself up to a little dumbshow whose flavor if not whose meaning was unmistakable. But I tried to ward off the meaning by continuing to speak about her even if speaking about her and the little ones and the trials and tribulations at hovel-side only convalidated that meaning.

Something in his position

Something in his position with relation to me recalled

Something in his position with relation to me recalled my position with relation to her. Or was this too easy an infliction of meaning on myself. Looking out to sea and as if parrying the blows of an invective directed elsewhere he reminded me of myself, standing outside the hovel as she berated me for my goats. Yes, he was experiencing the very same thing for by scraping his foot along the edge of the path leading to the very edge of the cliff he was telling me as much, namely, that his relation to me as I droned on about her and how she weighed me down was the mirror image of my relation to her. A peculiar slueing amid the scraping added that now he was the patient forbearing listener as all along I had prided myself on being with her. The crashing waves below echoed—codified—his meaning which in its final form suggested something to the effect that through an inevitable process and one by no means unique in the annals of rehabilitation my primary purpose in seeking him out or delivering myself up to the opportunity that perhaps unbeknownst to himself he offered—to wit, seamless excoriation of the one keeping me from the rocks and unending proclamation of our radical and ghastly difference in outlook—had given rise to an unforeseen and unforeseeable side effect, namely, an even more radical and ghastly indistinguishability between that one and me. What she was to me I had become for him. Here we were, then, she and I, alone at last, alone as we had never been when she berated me for what her symptom perceived to be mine and I strove to dodge her blows, alone at last and conflated—and in the course of the very process set aside to erect our indefeasible differences—conflated to the same behemoth. So this was what going-to-goat meant. Still turned away to the sea he was continuing his dumbshow. In fact if I didn't finally take it upon myself to turn away as a sign that I had had just about enough he would have continued to pile proof upon proof all in the name of this now established fact, unit of meaning, come to strengthen my story and thereby undo me. His every gesture went on demonstrating that in publicly lamenting her lamentations in the face of my vagrancies I only succeeded in transforming him into my self at the height of its manly forbearance while she and I of course went on to conflate ourselves into this now legendary behemoth. This was what going-to-goat meant.

Finally Herr Goat spoke, that is to say, he redistributed the weight of his haunches and lowered his chin to peck at a shaft of bluish fern. He did not raise his head for a long long while. This picking aimlessly at a shaft of fern followed by the refusal to look up and listen could only mean, Be more affectionate to the old sow. I felt compelled to remind him of how prodigally she expressed contempt for the way I dressed, smelled, navigated. He shrugged: and from between his hind legs hard little pellets emerged. This meant: Then tell her she has no right to be humiliating you if humiliation is what you think it is. How explain there was no expecting me to be broadly affectionate and then, out of the grey, put my foot down her throat and remind her nobody but nobody, did she hear nobody, had a right to put his foot down mine. There was simply no elasticizing our relation to compass these extremes. He gamboled off a few paces as if abandoning me for good: He did not understand nor did he care. It was then—as he extended his tail almost parallel with the ground—I deduced he was turning away in sadness. Seeing him look off every now and then as if recruiting others, any others, to share his outrage at a perfect stranger daring to eat up his precious time, I cried out that no one was more concerned about exploiting him than I. How convince him of how overwhelmed I was by my loathsome and obstructive paltriness faced with his godlike self-expenditure in my behalf. I looked back on myself in relation to him as all along he should have been looking. I looked back on my obliviousness to being looked at—sized up—found out—not so much with his eyes—for he did not have the heart, samaritan that he was! to look askance—as with the eyes of some enraged and impatient good companion and yoke-devil more protective of his welfare than he himself could ever be and righteously rightfully appalled at the mincemeat being made of his magnanimity. I looked back on myself, then, with the eyes of this all-seeing yoke-devil judging and damning me eternally for the complacency of an overweening insignificance obstructing the progress of one with an authentic stake in being. I kneeled down, began licking the grass: the only way available for showing my . . . pity. Yes, it was suddenly clear I was overwhelmed with pity for him, rather, for his *persistence in significant struggle though bereft of my potency.* Yes, at last I had found it in my heart to take pity on him as one of the infinitely many without my special gifts yet consigned to desiderate and struggle manfully in this world of orlops and oubliettes. I studied the blade of grass halfway in my mouth as if it could tell me in what consisted this special gift, this gramarye, this secret and clandestine *potency in another sphere.* Just as I was about to think: The sphere of the rocks, he turned abruptly around: Nothing could have prepared me for the sleek ferocity of this movement—more appropriate to a panther than to a goat—all the more so as it clearly meant, Imbecile! this charism—this

35

gladiolus-scented erogation of the lesser gods—is nothing more than a capacity to play dead at all times, to say no to all striving. And yet you feel guilty and apologetic for having been blessed with such a distinct advantage over all your fellows. And at the same time you envy their— my—infinitely greater strength in being able to survive without this advantage. He circled round me. I did not understand why. Hadn't I confessed to the limit of my powers. Was he seeking additional apologies for my secret but undeserved fund of strength. He began to gallop, following what seemed an elliptical course: It was only after nine revolutions that I understood what he was saying over and over— namely, that I must not feel as if I was exploiting him. By the thirteenth revolution his hoofs had sketched a flawless and exact version of my predicament: I was darkly uncertain whether it was my private secret fund of strength and contingency-free connectedness to the nether fonts of creative power or my bulky putrefactive insignficance that gave me no right to burden him, dogear the pages of his book of hours. And it was precisely this uncertainty that clamored for—required—vindicated—his help. Somewhere along the line this construction had refuted itself. Now that he had made it clear that I was saddled with a serious problem I felt free to confront the rocks. And they were not so far from where I stood as I initially thought. After my first look I turned away quickly because I could sense him, behind, appraising. His appraisal, if appraisal it was, was meant kindly, of that I was sure, meant, Go on, go on, look, get your feet wet, drown, resurface. I turned back, secure in the knowledge that he was both watching and watching out for me and that his watching in and of itself meant, Yes, go on, look look look and long for the fissure-clogged rock faces. This, my little friend, is what it means to be relapsed to the same craving with each relapse undergone as more unspeakable than the one before. Yet, as I was completing my turn—from him back to the rocks—I could it hear buzzing in my ears and by now it—my turn—no longer meant, Thanks for standing by, but rather, But, Herr Goat, Herr Goat, I never imagine them when I am away from them, I never think of them except when I am approaching. I never reconstruct them from scattered parts noted, craved, and ultimately unknown, fused now into some writhing supercentaur. So, Herr Goat, I am not quite the lazar your treacly ministrations take him for—

take me for—I am only intermittently roweled by this craving that dares not speak its name. So stop plastering me with your labels. I turned completely around now, to make my case stronger with the whole weight of my body.

He was chewing a shoe, one of mine. I knew even before looking all the way down. Where had I lost, relinquished it. The chewing meant

NO

The chewing meant

NO

It was only when he had spat out the shoe, laces and all, and in the general direction of the most enticing rock faces that at once I knew the chewing to mean, So, you determine this absence of a single feature—some farflung tendency to construct ideal rocks in their absence from remembered dismembered shards—to be the definitive proof of immunity to a craving that subsumes all such tendencies yet brazenly is not reducible to any. Has it never occurred to you that you may simply—or not so simply—be at a preliminary stage and have not yet achieved the courageous freedom to give yourself to this tendency, to allow yourself in the comfort of your parlor, let us say, to evoke and construct vanishingly ideal surfaces overrun with those clogged fissures to which, as I understand it, the smooth and undulating surfaces can never be reconciled, from which they recoil, yet which they flaunt with all the curule pomp at their disposal.

As he spoke he moved away or I moved away and continued moving away for this kind of thought—that for all its anti-blandishment I was still taking to be an exculpatory thought insofar as it proclaimed that I never found myself thinking about the rocks when far enough away, had never been responsible for strained and fabricated collocation of remembered shards for the purpose of producing the ideal ectype, had never invoked them to supply the empyrosis missing from our rare moments of what is familiarly known as conjugal intimacy [the little ones across the partition avid of course for any telltale signs]—for this kind of thought is the kind of thought that, before and during the thinking as well as long after, tends to propel one away from the vicinity of living beings for such a vicinity will only require further clarification of *this kind of thought.* One thinks such a thought or coerces another into thinking for one and before one knows it one has moved away, far far away, from the site of its eruption. He went on chewing in the stark absence of something to chew and the chewing meant, went on meaning, that under no circumstances was I to think that this exculpatory thought about an exculpatory nontendency proved I had not reached, had not allowed myself to reach, was nowhere near reaching, a more advanced stage—almost impressionistic—of the craving that was still, never fear, loudly incubating within. The chewing also meant he was well aware of my efforts to move away from my exculpatory thought at the same time that I was holding on to it for dear life in spite of its jumble of unwanted implications. Just when I was beginning to hunger to remark to someone or something that our relation—our connection—was well-nigh over, so one-sided and recriminatory had it become, I found he was still galloping after me. He charged toward me over the little stones: A few little pelletlike shits emerged from his shriveled hindquarters in the fever of advance. Coming, as goats will and must do, to a standstill a few inches from my groin, which he proceeded to smell noncommittally, that is to say, paraprofessionally, he hiccoughed. I waited. I did not want the hiccough to mean, to be decipherable, translatable, even if the translation was already galloping toward me. The hiccough most definitely did mean, for it responded perfectly to the importunities of this time and place. He had found a name for his state, which was what was left over when all the importunities were subtracted from the rest of being as we were knowing—helping to constitute—it here and now and the hiccough was that name. Suddenly I was sick of a world where there is never the least danger of not finding the right name for the fumarole belching, the mofette spiraling; where everything no matter how untowardly erupting—the more untowardly the better—finds its right name double quick or has a right name found for it and therefore is no longer either untoward or erupting. Sick, sick, sick of this world—his world—a goat's world—in the shape of a quasi-rational solidarity-ridden old fart synthesized without surcease as weasel paean to all this unendingly smiling accommodation of words to things and things to words.

He was not aware of this supreme moment of discovery. He was still too busy with the hiccough meaning and not only did it mean immediately but it looked as if it might very well be going on meaning and meaning and meaning more and more for quite some time. Right now I knew what it meant: Don't stay here. Go back to your rocks. You can resolve your craving for the rocks only within the context of the rocks, that is, in the vicinity of the vicinity of their vicinity. Abstention from the rocks, which all decked out in your sanbenito you are practicing now—a tyro stylite atop the caryatid of my protection—is not a sign of strength, or rather, whatever strength accrues has only a momental resonance within the overall context of enslaved weakness. You must return to the rocks: the bald and the beautiful. The only viable— conceivable—activity within the context of the rocks is . . . craving for the rocks. He blinked a little perversely, I thought, as if to say, Whoever *that* is.

I heard all this in a single key, that of his absolute refusal to treat my despair. It was easy for him, a goat, a mere goat with access to the rocks any time he desired, to suggest a return to their realm. He was forgetting that I had the little woman and the little ones and their symptoms as well as countless other abandoned matters to contend with. All of a sudden the rocks had derogated from the very core of my being to a feeble parergon of his invention. I squatted, wounded by his frivolity, thought I heard a sound. The further off I moved the surer I became that the sound had not come from him. Looking back I saw he had moved. I had taken his movement for a sound maybe because it was so overresonant with his previous certainty that giving myself freely to the rocks would be in the long run salutary. The way he deftly skipped aside in the now wide distance between as I made an ineffectually menacing movement toward his general direction sketched the remote possibility for our connection of a *new beginning*, a different key, of, say, solicitude. But did I want solicitude at this late date? What could solicitude do but destroy the densifying cohesion of a burgeoning world view subsuming rocks and goats and far far more than rocks and goats? At this point wouldn't solicitude be far more debilitating than his blunt refusal to commend my refusal to collaborate joyfully in what I had suddenly taken to calling—just this very minute—my brute exploitation by the rocks, lofty leaden things born to grind alien nisus to nothingness. He was part of the world external to my anguish and as part of that world it was preferable that he play its tune. From the way voluptuously he raised a hoof to the rays of the setting sun it occurred to me that he was probably revolted not by my relation to—craving for—the rocks per se—whatever *that* was—but by the failure to promise even dimly a beginning and an end to its drama capable of offering, so it would seem, only a dimwitted succession of upsurging failed peripeties forever steering—or veering—clear of anything stinking however vaguely of the bright moral lesson.

I was willing to do anything to avoid the rocks: sorely tempted to begin telling him their story as our story from the very beginning. Could I begin legitimately beginning long before or after the point where that story might take it into its head to jump head first into the caldron of meaning thereby unleashing so much displaced ooze upon the world of knowing listeners already greedily slobbering for more. I began to begin, hoping to reach the end, hoping there would be an end to reach. But then he twisted his hoof in the direction of another sunset. This meant unequivocally that our meeting was over and done with. Then he twisted back in my direction, that of sunset's bloody death, favorite of tourists. This meant it was time to begin. So he was sharply reducing the interval between our sessions. But where had I derived the notion of a fixed interval, a protocol in danger of violation. Time to resume but with what since in the interval between the hoof's twisting away and twisting back there had been no exploitable incidents. . . . to propel forward the story I had to tell. But what was all this talk about incidents: The story I had to tell and for which he was waiting did not need supplementary incidents dragged in from who knows where. Only I needed them, precisely because they had nothing to do with the story, could only postpone and replace it. So here we were arrived at yet another session, spewed out of yet another interval defined by one hoof twisting this way and another twisting that and thirsty for story. Yet all I could think about and lament was the absence of incidents liberated by this interval and capable of giving me a grip on, foothold in, the story, that is, of successfully abolishing its claims on his time and my transformative self-loathing. The session was going forward—inexorably—before I could mask the everpresent subjacent story matter blessedly insusceptible to the upsurge of telling as event—with incident, details of marginal and unsymptomatic collision with this or that papery jutting along the cliffs.

Here I was confronted with yet another session but not, fortunately or unfortunately, with another goat: always the same goat, Herr Goat, fixed at the same threshold of livid expectation—confronted with yet another session [defined as postlude to a hoof's turning away and turning back] yet bereft of any incidents to camouflage the story subsidizing the session and distract from the terror of having nothing to say—nothing to tell—but that story's amorphous pullulating subjacency. How begin to tell what was just and infinitely beneath the missed recounting of an incident that should have existed in the interval between a hoof's turning away and back. Yet it was unclear what he, the same goat, wanted. Did he want in fact the story of my connection to the rocks—one with beginning, middle, and end, as if susceptibility to cure could be directly correlated with its—the story's—beribboned framing for holiday consumption? Or did he want the slaver of incidents? Or was he stoically holding out for a bumbling presentation of the terrifying subjacent in its sheer amorphousness of writhing cursing recoil from all brotherly intervention? Was the last rehabilitation's key? And was that her advancing on us from a great distance, the little ones trailing behind, this one distracted by the sky, that one by the ochrous rock faces ingathering.

The goat did not seem concerned perhaps because from the other direction a little troupe of kindred was advancing. He turned to smile at them. With a forehoof he directed them to where they must stand in readiness. One of the troupe—they had formed an ellipse— withdrew from the closed curve into the waning, almost whimpering, sunlight. This movement meant: My chief was interested in you at a particular moment in your waking life. He allowed space in time for the question I refused to ask: What moment. This adjutant's withdrawing even further now into the whimpering background meant: You were emerging from among the rock faces—a site with which you at all cost did not wish to be identified. You were intent only on escape but something changed: A look of woe flitted across your face. My goat, Herr Goat, looked hard at his junior colleague then hard—even harder

NO—hard at me. The succession of looks meant: For you discovered you might have lost something. What was it you feared having lost and may, for all we know, have lost: we will never know. All we can say for sure: The more precious the object in question the more irrevocable the loss.

The goats waited as if for a cue. He furnished it: scratched his buttocks with a dew claw. Another goat exited from the ellipse then returned, moving toward a point within roughly equidistant from the two foci. Herr Goat caught my eye as if to reinforce the meaning, already self-evident, of this exit and return: You went back, to the rock faces, their annihilating fissures now swathed in purplish shadow. You made the effort to go back—I'll say that for you—but it was only in a kind of frenzy, to stave off the inevitable moment when you must be alone with your loss, that you went back in, into the crevices, to demand—Is that too strong a word?—that the flashlight of dusk be conscientiously trained across the area in which you had communed— Is that too weak a word?—with your congeners. In other words, going back to the den to confirm that status of the lost object was only a way of deferring the moment of loss, already long passed into history, moment of resignation to loss, capitulation to the torture of loss engi-neered by some monstrous other all along waiting in the wings of your craving proven violent and uncontrollable—some incarnated stealth casually prowling the surface of your being but never in the service of that being—some embodied nonbeing made to the measure of an un-derstandably frenzied dispossession in the face of gigantic fissures chocked full of hair and other tantalizing exuviae—some Grendel on the chthonian lookout for the moment proper to a gliding in on your overproclaimed quivery-thighed euphoria.

He stopped, although I could not remember his having started, looked around. He clearly wanted this image of the goats all in a circle, or rather, all but one in a circle, or rather, in an ellipse, with one toward the core and equidistant from both foci and the exception out some-where stalking the gorse and timothy at their most mephitic, to continue, to persist as permanent and most plausible source of what he had to say. Alas, he knew this particular image had petered out. As if responding to his torment the goatlet situated between the two foci moved to coincide with one of them. He, my goat, Herr Goat, shook his beard from relief for this was a sign that a new image had been generated enabling him to go on: You went back, I say, to the site of sites, although in the damp glow charily—almost anathematizingly—doled out to the weary traveler compliments of Twilight Kilowattage, Ltd., you could not quite distinguish the site in question, the site of loss, the site whence all that was most precious had oozed. And when you did at last distinguish the site or some reasonable facsimile thereof immediately it became the prior therefore rightful site of the perpetrator of that loss. He now made a jerkily deictic gesture in the general direction of that goat who had had the decency, tact, quickwittedness, to adopt the point of view of a focus in a time of great need. Even if both of you could have managed to occupy the same site at the same time it was now irrefutably his—its—site. All of a sudden Quick Witted seemed to have grown Disgusted for without a single prior sign of discontent he had managed to leap outside the ellipse and join his estranged colleague among the fuming stinking alfalfa, bindweed, gorse, heather, and privet. Grinding his jaws in their direction Herr Goat made me understand I was compelled to believe in a perpetrator whether or not there was one. The agony of loss simultaneously— therapeutically—had brought forth an embodied slyness lurking somewhere in its shrubbery even if that embodied slyness was nothing more and nothing less than my own forgetfulness and frenzy or rather, my craving's forgetfulness and frenzy in the face of the . . . faces. Seeking a correlative that frenzied forgetfulness deep inside forgetful frenziedness—rocks inside the goats and goats inside the rocks, to quote my biggest little one—had come up with the monstrous other consecrated to robbing me of my most precious possession. Rather than own up to a simple loss of self to hog-wild craving I preferred to fabricate the ravishing posture of a *most precious object*, a prized possession, and lay its fictive loss at the doorstep of a sly invidious ravager equally fictive though far more vigilant.

Though not very far away they were taking an inordinately long time reaching us. There were no unsuspected declivities and hair's-breadth defiles to justify an elapse of time that seemed endless. Maybe what took them so long was her constantly turning around to berate the little ones, who did not take kindly to whatever she said. They stamped, a bit like goats. And then in the midst of her fury which, knowing her, was more than a simple fury alloyed as it must be with the fury of having her initial and, as she believed, impregnable fury fleered at by the little ones—she saw the goat. He was making gestures with his tail and his beard not at all compatible, I brightly suspected, with the demands of a symptom which, to judge by her ataxia, was still in its horrific heyday. She squinted hard at his hoofs, his shiny coat, his jutting jaw, his scrawny chest—all the secondary sexual paraphernalia vindicating the shrillness of the symptom—but it was clear hers was a seeing without seeing, a seeing incapable of emerging from the fortress—the fastness—of its fury. And this was the kind of fury that renders attainment of a perception unobstructed by its own promptings inconceivable. She was doomed to see what she wanted to see: what the symptom deemed she needed to see. And so—always judging from her ataxia and regular outlashings at the kiddies not quite taken in tow—this resistance on the part of her seeing to what in fact it did see of the goats and me and the relation of them to me and me to them—this refusal of a seeing purged of the premeditation of a secret and fuliginous bile—all this resistance and all this refusal was fast producing a phenomenon—an incident—that was neither goats-and-me nor her seeing of goats-and-me and least of all a compromised and weighted average of the two—least of all and never that—but rather a qualitative leap into another dimension. Her blocked—her dereistic inner seeing of what in her infinite futility of pride she took to be The Goat(s) was managing to gain admittance for all concerned into this other dimension which, incidentally, forswore any truck with goats, ithyphallic or otherwise, as well as those who crave them through no fault—or choice—of their own.

This was the final flowering, then, of what I had been long experiencing as her unseeing seeing. She had all along been seeing the goats, me, me among the goats, the goats in me, without seeing. For hers was a symptomed seeing. Yet having taken her unseeing seeing to its illogical conclusion—having refused all along until this bitter end to deballast that typically outraged and omniscient seeing of its symptomal pre- and misconceptions—she was free at last, like a child that has bawled itself to sleep, sleep a little to the side of itself, of its usual self, the self that makes it a point to apperceive every object and every event as inevitable extrusion of its clawing want. She was transformed. Or was I, in so praising her transformation, simply throwing a little raw meat of placation in the direction of the story's feeding time. I moved toward the goat. He turned to his kindred, made some uncapturable gesture then turned back to me. His belly expanded. All or some of this meant that he understood and even shared my hope. But was it hope I was experiencing. At any rate as she approached—closer and closer and closer— I saw that the demeaning and vindictive ataxia was still upon her. Nothing was changed.

I moved toward the ellipse; barely tangent to its circumference I looked in her direction as if to say, I abstain, I abstain. I do not enter. I cried out: I abstain. I abstain. But one of the goats—in an almost diametrically opposite position—neighed as if begging me to stop. I shared his sentiments. I resented having to expend this dumbshow of abstention on the goats, with whom I had never been involved in a way that made abstention—must less undying protestations of same—meaningful to the rabid ear. But the goat—my goat—Herr von Goat—did not care toward whom or what abstention was directed. It was the concept in its nudity that interested him. For his heuristic convenience he had no trouble transplanting said concept in its nudity to present circumstances. By kicking up a little storm of dirt he signaled that it was time for the goats to disperse in all directions but hers, for she was still advancing, still fleered at by the little ones. After they had indeed dispersed—a few, I might add, disobeying his instructions—he turned back to me, waiting. I too was waiting until I finally understood all he had had any intention of saying was siphoned off into instructions to the dispersing herd. I played them back.

They meant: As my confessor he was obliged to let me know it was in my very best interest to confess, never mind what, whether goats in rocks or rocks in goats or me in rocks and goats or goats and rocks in me. Much better to confess than abstain and make heavy weather out of abstaining. And how make heavy weather of such a bruised and pitiful entity, by its nature minutely circumstantial. Whereas, surrender to the unspeakable craving at last confessed, auditors, confessors, interlocutors, bystanders, coadjutors, mufti, dragomen, accessories before and after the fact, could not but be completely effaced in the tidal wave of a telling of that authentic surrender. Didn't I know—his stare was particularly intense at this point in my retrospection even if not by any stretch of the imagination directed my way—that the paroxysm dreaded and damned was never localizable at any particular moment in the playing out of the craving—the hunger—the desire—but long before: at the actual moment of choosing to surrender undergone as the active and shameless interment of a hunger to abstain.

He nibbled on a few leaves of timothy. Although I cannot say for sure whether timothy is leafed. Diminishing in intensity and as if no longer serving a trophic function, the nibbling was giving me to understand that I might take as long as I liked to grasp what it had bodied forth in its heyday of a few minutes before. Gradually—no longer distracted by a memory of his chomping jaws and salivating teeth and foul breath—I understood at last that the nibbling comprised not only a proleptic alertness to my certain bafflement at all this talk about surrender being superior to abstention but the very stuff and matter of a doing away forever with that bafflement. I listened long, I listened hard: And why is everyone and everything from the burliest policeman down to the wispiest gnat effaced in the tidal bore of actual entry into the true home of your craving? Why is descent into the iniquity of the unspeakable ultimately cleaner and purer than abstention?—why does it give one [although one should not of course be concerned with such matters at the point of entry] a decided advantage with respect not only to the one to whom one has the misfortune to be confessing but also to those infinite others to whom in a million years one would never dream of confessing. Why is it infinitely preferable—infinitely more empowering—to say, I entered, as opposed to, I wandered around for hours, incapable of eluctating out of the miasma of futile debate, reduced to counting the number of hexagonal tiles fringed with wilted begonias separating me from my endpoint. I could not answer, especially as she and the little ones were almost upon us. This was neither the time nor place for dimestore lucidity.

He turned in their direction, with a certain theatrical melancholy. Why, why, why, his sighing look said. I'll tell you why. To say, point blank: I came, I saw, I entered, is to ally oneself with the alien medium—the cave, the den, the ingathering of rock faces roasting in the sun—aginst the listener, against all listeners, and to subjugate them completely, no matter how much strength they seem to be entitled to draw from disapproval. The brute ability to have chosen overrides what was chosen—flouts whatever stench appears to enanate from that alien medium in which he, the chooser, chose to find himself at last.

He sensed some uneasiness, maybe even some demurral, for he stretched his neck toward me or toward something beyond me. At any rate the stretching was welcome for it meant, Yes, yes, yes, nice of you to have scruples about putting something over on your listener. For there is a certain boldness accruing to the confession of entry which boldness may or may not have been ingredient in—was probably not ingredient in—the entry qua entry. So what if the boldness comes first to birth in the telling. The telling is the crucial element here.

I had no alternative but to scratch my leg, which tried to mean: Remember when you spoke about the paroxysm residing in the actual choosing and not in whatever was subsequent to the choosing as a deployment—an outlay of the craving. There was no need to scratch any further for he was already erupting with knowing giggles most conspicuously concentrated in his shoulders. Of course I remember, of course I remember. But all this business about the paroxysm residing here instead of there and not here but there—that is not necessarily true out in the world, the world of, for example, your craving for—your craving among—the rocks. This is to say, who knows if the authentic paroxysm takes place precisely at—is indistinguishable from—the dark moment of choosing finally to enter. When you finally decide to enter the ring of rocks you may not experience anything even vaguely resembling a paroxysm. But here and now, where it is always and only a question of the recuperative telling of a doing, whether or not the doing was done, it is the flow of the actual telling that determines what is or is not true. At any rate, bold telling of bold choosing to enter boldly belongs to a single country—the country of strength—whereas abstention and its telling belong to no country—neither the alien medium nor the reprobating other—yet are reprehensible in both.

She was almost arrived, surrounded not only by the clamoring little ones but by the goats that, defying their master, had gone out to meet if not greet her. She was taking a certain pleasure in having all this attention, as if it lent a certain weight to her descent upon my negligence. I cried out: The event! the event! More than descent into the ring of rocks she is the event. His groin twitched in such a way as to suggest, more than suggest, sketch outright, the imperative, Shape it: shape the event. Though suddenly when he used the word I hadn't the faintest idea to what it could possibly refer. There were no events, never had there been any events, I had all along been mercilessly stymied in my quest for events to abolish the terrifying monotony of our sessions which, to the bargain, had followed one so quickly on the heels of its predecessor that I was incessantly left amorphous and deep in the mangy marl of event's total absence forever threatened by the invasion of that subjacent purulence that was my story though too monolithically inbred to succumb to the elements of story, the analgesia of incident, of event.

Turning from me to her, he sniffed at this advance festooned with fanfares and acclamations. Then I understood—from him—since I had enormous trouble understanding directly from myself given that my understanding, that is to say, my labeling, of whatever it was I professed to understanding label was in the service of annihilation or, at the very least, the permanent impounding of what could very well turn out to be yet another plaything of others' percipience to be turned ultimately against me—then I understood—from him—as he sniffed at this advance festooned with this and that—then I understood that she was the event. She was the event, or rather, the event was her coming. I saw no way of shaping this event and said as much, in his language of course, by standing a little to one side of his sniffing with my legs crossed and my fingers up my nose. She was still a long way off although this preternatural slowness could in no way be explained by the obstacle of immense distances.

I saw no way of shaping the event and said as much, right now, by standing off even a little further and relieving myself *as in the old days*. Although once the need to utter had been satisfied I had to confess myself baffled by the phrase. Did it refer to the old days of my first meeting with Herr Goat? old days of my life with her and the little ones? old days of my life before her? old days of the accursed womb? The smell brought me back to myself or rather brought me back another being entirely—all too familiar, unwelcome, cloying therefore invincible against all buffets. For the self that relieved itself was not the self of my glorious misconceptions.

He was watching me again. Did this mean she was too close for the comfort of sniffing? The intensity of the watching meant: The event. Shape it. As a man would shape it. I wiped my buttocks *in a certain manner*, without paper, foliage, without fingers even, for this was my only way of beginning to signify a reply. The only antidote, so stated an especially stalwart upward wiping stroke, against the event—as if his jussive, almost military, tone had any concern with antidote—the only antidote is not to assert my potent—my indomitable—presence in the midst—at the very core—of event. I died here. So far I was immensely satisfied with my strokes as a form of goatish expression though hardly with their efficacy as a means of ridding me of excrement. He lowered his head, to punish me, and so I had no choice but to go on: The only antidote against event—against the encroachment of event—is event's inevitability—the fact that it has to descend and descending has also to end. So in the long run it is only event—not me—only event—that can spare me having to shape event. Only event—rather, the inevitability, the sluggish imminence, the imminent inevitable extinction of event in its own bloody imminence—extinction of event in the face, that is, of my definitively hopeless and helpless efforts to shape it—rescue it—only event itself unrescued by me can, in turn, rescue me.

Making a spyglass lens of my fingers I looked out in their general direction. The children were weeping. They looked painfully neglected, not so much in their habitus or raiment as in their general outlook, their sharply diminished capacity for pleasurable expectation. A lashing rain was deadening their features though the air was perfectly clear and shot through with the most unexceptionable sunshine. Seeing them in such disrepair spurred me to resume wiping the hairy old cleft so as to be able to communicate as rapidly as possible: The problem with shaping the event is that said shaping is indistinguishable from shaping the players trapped inside the event, reorienting their inherent capacity for malicious destruction. And although from bitter past experience I know there is nothing more futile and repercussive than to be taken *au dépourvu* it is somehow far more unbearable—as least as long as one is perched on its far side—as I always manage to be—even long after all is said and done—to entrench myself in the event before the event. To mold the event proleptically and prophylactically is to live the event twice, sometimes three times. In addition—such is the anti-nature of its ever-changing intricacies of internal process—giving to its infinite details the infinite attention they deserve can easily be confused with a hopeless floundering among the event—not only by bystanders but by the perpetrator himself.

She was here at last. The little ones wandered about. No pretending she was still en route. I stood still though I was always standing still. The event—her coming, her advance, her reproach, her testimony, her well-founded exasperation, her cogent loathing, her martyred revulsion, her justified impatience—was inevitably through the fetor of its momentum—like the soothing glide of an odorless fart over the searing itch of a hemorrhoid—and willy-nilly about to sweep me up into its inexorable sludging trek toward extinction. By ostentatiously smelling those stinking fingers assigned the unholy task of absterging my cleft— though with absolutely no reproach intended toward my confessor for not providing the appropriate implements if implements there were in these parts—I managed to iterate: The only antidote for event—event afferent—is its inevitability, that is to say, its extinction bringing to a halt—superseding—effecting deconstruction of—this the immense groined vault of my incapacity to shape it. I hid myself to pull up my trousers, lower my shirt. Hiding myself even if there was no place to hide myself meant: So I am staying put.

She recoiled in disgust from the space between the goat and me. He made a rasping sound with his hoof against a nearby rock and his myriad kindred hurried over all in a leap to fill the space in question. I could not identify the form they created. Would she be able to read that form? I looked at her eagerly hoping she would manage to understand for I understood just enough to know the form worked to my detriment and must therefore endear them—Herr Goat and his kind—to her. Look at him, the form said, standing still or wanting to, overcome with a certain misery of impatience, optimism even, as if this is autumn and he the schoolboy anticipating a new term's surprises—an optimistic impatience, then, to leap into the future incarnated in the inevitable unfolding, that is to say, extinction, of the event as compacted specimen daily grind—as if by leaping into the future he cannot help but accelerate its—the event's—or the future's, for that matter—progress toward extinction, that is to say, annihilation, that is to say, transmogrification into the miraculous charism that is not just reparation for but retroactive undoing of every single flagitious moment of that progress. Clearly he is forgetting that minutes—years—centuries of brute duration comprising just such untransmogrified, untransmogrifiable, events as—this, her righteous forward march advancing spreadeagled on the bier of his culpability and in the company of those needy spotless little ones forever branded by neglect and bad example—that years—centuries—millennia—have successfully resisted just such transmogrification—have managed adroitly to sidestep contamination by somebody's or some thing's craving for transformation of sedimentary, igneous, or metamorphic routine into its better. As if routine as brute duration and vice-versa had the sensorimotor equipment to begin tiring of itself—as if brute routine comprising the infinite succession of pug-nosed events indistinguishable each from the other could be contaminated by his excruciated sentiency—his exacerbated erithism—and is, this brute duration of routine, anything but an insensate plowing unregenerate and unabashed through the heart of organism after organism. She advanced toward me as the goats departed. They saluted each with his hind legs at a certain juncture. She did not notice. And this not noticing, with she and they, both potent forces, locked—at that pregnant moment of her not-noticing—in the frame of my attention, was invested with the acutest pathos, almost resuscitated her as a life partner. The forthrightness of her delicate movements intended for my direction—the way she adjusted her cadogan, her reticule—yes, for a split second, she was emerging from my true home, the nineteenth-century novel—yet all overlaid with this unconsciousness of their—the hind legs'—obeisance in her favor—this disjunction between infinite grace in disarray and infinite unconsciousness—this emancipation from an insidious vigilance ultimately sluggish and lumpishly earthbound—transformed her into one irresistible because unrecognizable.

You went with him, she said, nodding in the direction of the dear departing, more of a goatherd than a goat. Now the event was upon me, dreaded and abhorred, though showing no signs of disintegration. Not answering, I looked over her head and the heads of the little ones to my goatherd—Herr Goatherd—who seemed, rubbing his pastern against the floor of his latent udder or grazing his left stifle with his front knee, to be saying: The event is here. Stop pretending it isn't here yet by concentrating only on its refusal to be gone. And the other goats, by not so much mimicking these gestures as turning toward the setting rock faces flavid in the rising light, repeated: The event is here. Long live the event. I'm here, she said, even though you went with a goat. I had forgotten the sound of the human voice.

I had choices. I could wait for her to speak or assume she had already spoken the following: I am here, the event you were waiting for. Only when was the likes of you able to live an event: For the likes of you event begins only after you have abused and contused it. Only then does the event begin—but as a rectification of the prior non-event. Only in expiation do you have a strong enough goad to falling through the incontinent lap of event.

I had choices. I could respond as if she had already spoken that following or expostulate with her for having not. I waited for her to go on.

I waited for her to go on: I hadn't succumbed to either the first or second set of choices, second depending from an arm of the first. Did you intend to go back to the rocks? I did not know if I thought this recognition of the rocks a good sign. A good sign of what? What is a good sign? I answered: I have every intention of going back to the rocks. The rocks are my very own. God's own country and all that rot. Those hairy fissures: How resist? She shook her head, lulled by the newfound chastity of an understanding unblurred. I smiled, to suggest that even if I returned to the rocks this did not necessarily mean I would not return—might not like to return—to her and the little ones, besymptomed and in dire need of a father's caressing hand. The rocks are my life, I added, not sure if this proclamation leveled all previous efforts at reconciliation. The rock faces and only the rock faces encourage me to rise up in temerity of indignation whenever I am misprized. Until I remember there is nothing to fall back on—no *where* to fall back on. All the more reason for the rocks to constitute my life. Why—she spewed—

because they callously furnish no resting place? She looked like she could have spat volumes now the subject was the one she knew best—my misjudgments, my mismanagements. What about the little ones? They need you to fall back on something so they can fall back against you. She called to them, they had scattered, a few in the direction of the goats, others toward the rock faces, ruddy-cheeked and wholesomely inviting for a split second in this atypical slant of dusk. I did not know how to answer.

The way she scratched her hip meant—I was decoding her as if she were a goat—Direct your attention to something besides me. Forget about responding to—against—me. She was putting the needs of the story—mine—hers—ours—before her own. The story was anticipatorily exhausted by my efforts at plausible response to her reproaches. I could have said: Take me back, or, Come with me to the rocks and I'll bid for your initiation. Or better—or worse—Give me the little ones and I'll initiate them myself. As if in harmony with every stage of my vacillation she went on murmuring, The wonderful rocks. They stink. Did you know that. This comment produced an overwhelming craving to return to the rocks—to be among them once more, grazed by a crazed outrage and defiance—to be spilling the seed of my disaffection into their crevices, letting her and her little ones fend for themselves, symptoms or no symptoms. I stayed put. The wonderful rocks, I replied. So at last she was taking the connection seriously. But it would have been yet another terrible desecration of meaning to claim or even assume rocks had replaced goats in the *grimoire* of her symptoms. As the little ones scattered only to return, again and again and again, she surprised me by saying in a tone of total self-possession, So what have you learned at his side. There was no trace of the exertion of her symptom as she spoke, so calmly, of the goat, my goat, Herr Goat. This mention of Herr Goat put me in doubt of myself, which doubt took the form of doubt about Herr Goat. I wanted him nearby so that I could inventory his vital parts and thereby rest assured he was a goat, was still a goat. No, it wasn't that. I simply needed the goat, Herr Goat, a goat, a thing, some thing, some manifest sum of parts, even goatish ones, to oppose to the insidious mastery of her question or to help me bide the time of a response to it. Something in the question—presenting too much self-mastery [as too much goat] for my delectation and taking the ways of the world [as the ways of confessorial goat] far more seriously than I had ever thought of taking it—drove me to seek refuge—anywhere, in goat, say, as a sum of irrepressibly goatish parts. So is it any wonder that at this moment of a melancholy mastery new to her tone, suggesting that she wished to begin with me anew but in a completely different key signature, I should think about beginning to fix my attention on his tail, pinbone, thigh, flank, tendon, hock, pastern, hoof, dewclaw, heel, toe, sole, rump, back, loin, ribs, shine, crop, withers, neck, shoulder blade, car, poll, forehead, nose, nostril, muzzle, jaw, throat, dewlap, brisket, barrel, feathers, beak, gizzard, and crop, and so on and so forth to thurl and back again?

Her sidelong mention of my therapeutic relation to this creature celebrated for doing only good made me feel depleted of all justifiable claim on his attention. So here I was replenishing myself in the only way I knew how if not the only way open to me: via body parts. And at the same time this glancing reference suggesting a calm acceptance at last made me want to participate far more actively in what I had immediately distorted into a full-bodied, almost fulsome, enshrinement, to live more closely and more permanently in the warming shadow of the mangled thing enshrined. And the only way of participation was, again, inventory. Never had I so delectated—as I did now in their absence—over the withers rising imperceptibly above the crest of the shoulder blades. And so on and so forth. At the same time I had the feeling that this blazon of goatly virtues was nothing more than an inept and lackluster prosectomy aimed at staving off all further mention of the creature. As if further mention would be too painful or bring us to a dead end with nothing ever again to say about the goat or about all that was not goat. So to stave off this nothingness I went on *reminiscing* about how the thighs stood apart from the rear, allowing room for presentation of the udder, and how the top of the chine always managed—whatever the weather—to descend slightly, almost imperceptibly, from the withers in a single slope, and how the barrel, though wide and bellowing and deep, still blended beautifully with the rest of the body. For her benefit I was making, and successfully, so I thought, the goat's essence seem the result of hard work. So I went on, *remembering* how the goat, at the very moment when he was completely given up to choreographing the configuration of the herd, nevertheless remained completely faithful to the age-old practice [very much in danger of dying out] of advancing directly down on the hoof and not back on the dewclaw, a foulsmelling and functionless pedal digit. This memory naturally led me to that of the udder blending into the stomach on the belly without the slightest trace of a waterlogged runnel between stomach and udder, udder and stomach.

He has taught me to accept my connection to the faces *en bloc* and not to presume that my veering toward their lodestone is a mere stage in some progress upwards or downwards. I was afraid—and immediately played back what I had said even before it was out of my mouth—she would take this as some kind of reassurance that I would never be lost to her among the rocks. He has taught me to accept the rock faces as outside myself and not simply called into being at the behest of my confusion concerning just where I stand in relation to them, to the world. The little ones gathered round. They were cutting off my view of the faces, always stirring at that hour. Returning to the hovel we passed the goats: We had moved into their distance, no longer quite so grim. He was still their goatherd—their fugleman—their pendragon. But though they were still going through various conformations at an alarmingly virtuosic rate, he was no longer living through those conformations as forms through which he might communicate with me. His job was done, as far as he was concerned, as far as I was concerned, as far as the story was concerned, as far as the story's necessary desecration of the memory of meaning was concerned.

He was still living through those conformations as vital forms through which he might communicate with me and with those who had the misfortune to come after.

His job was not done, as far as he was concerned.

I was waiting for her to speak of the rock faces, unsure if they would remain real after she spoke of them, if they were real since she hadn't yet spoken of them. They drew back, puckered, pinkish, lastingly wounded by all they had witnessed at what had been imposed upon them as their *site*—something about one hog pursued by another and returning to the trough in a panic of dreaded loss. They drew back as if still bristling at the reproaches heaped upon them somewhere in the course of my sessions with Herr Goat. What is there left for us, I could not help asking emboldened by the undulating faces subtly fissured and clogged dwindling in the distance. What do you mean, she replied, trying to evict grudgingness from her tone and succeeding only partially. I still want the rock faces to the exclusion of all else. Then go to your goats and to the exclusion of all else.

The little ones laughed convulsively when they caught my eye and even when they no longer caught it because it was caught elsewhere went on giving way to the same genial paroxysms it should have engendered.

Remember, the symptom is the form anxiety takes when said anxiety persists, needs to persist, in believing itself only temporary, just passing through. On the other hand, recognition of anxiety's inexhaustibility can never be equivalent to its abolition. So, if after all recognition isn't to be rewarded by cure, why bother admitting to anxiety in the first place?

—*Auntie Goat in a phone call to The Anti-Goat,*
ca. Forty-fifth century, B.C.

Goat Song 2

I must speak of the rocks and the goats, though I am not particularly well suited to discuss either. But I must begin even if every time I am about to begin *somewhere* I feel that I am formulating what is merely the best because most accessible camouflage of what should have been brought forth. So what I end up bringing forth is not my relation to the rocks nor hers to the goats but basest subterfuge, so much sand thrown in the eye of event that might have been.

At any rate, she was armed only and exorbitantly with a symptom decreeing my promiscuity among various species of goat. While I was fighting with some thing struggling to accede to the status of symptom and not quite focused on the rock faces near our hovel. For we were poor folk if not quite poor in symptoms.

One morning—mornings—off I went, the sky busy with cumulus, that is, supercharged with the revelations of a still-to-be-decoded script. But I did not—never—had the patience to listen for I was on my way—forever on my way—to the rocks and my anticipation so unnerved, unmanned, and exalted me that there was no putting stock in anything that was not rock and had no intention ever of becoming rock.

I knew she had eyes only for my next encounter with the goats, surely not my first and not to be my last. I could hear her behind me. There was no escape before the ravine where miraculously and due to I know not what deformity, either hers or the landscape's, I managed to elude her. Although overwhelmed by relief at this modest compensation for the torment engendered by her having been hot in pursuit during the early stages of my journey I was nevertheless aghast and saddened to find myself once again at the mercy of the eternal bookkeeper who if allowing me now to lose her had made sure to exact the dues of prior torment and then some. And what was my only defense against this fixed and rotting state of affairs but a thought, that is to say, a measly contingency born of contingency.

My excuse before leaving the house and the little ones was that I was off in search of a job that did not fall into the freelance mode. She was after all sick to death of the freelancer in me. It's true: she had had a bellyful over the years. One would think having once informed her of how I intended to spend the day I should, in anticipation of the rocks, be walking on air. Unfortunately, this fiction of a search for the freelance position worthy of her expectations generated far more of an urgency of further accretions of alibi than I, beshrewn recrement, knew how to overrule. Although not quite able to determine my relation to this fiction—Was it a fiction? create? imminent? posthumous?—I knew I simply could not accept it for what it would have liked me to take it to be: masterly gammon in the face of her suspicions. No belief in my powers as a confidence man. What I had invoked as a ploy, an emanation from within, was something circumstantial and unattainable assaulting from without.

In short, I desperately envied this freelancer scrupulously in search of his full-time job, certain she must prefer him to me. I envied not just him but every detail of his life; serene management of woman and little ones, ability to keep his chin up to reconciling boondoggle and pursuit of the highest pursuits. I envied every detail of his life that was pretty much every detail of my life but with the sign reversed. What I— amid my penetralia—underwent as loathsome obstructions to communion with the rocks and whatever lay beyond or behind or within was now—in him, from him—the enterprising freelancer with never an unkind word for anybody—were now the bludgeoning and inextirpable fixtures of a luminous teleology. I loathed myself for loathing what was turning out—what had turned out—to be crucial to his—the other's— somebody's—achievement. Consequently, search for a full-time job and craving for the rocks had not—as I had hoped—revealed themselves to be mutually exclusive. They were two very much nonmutually exclusive phenomena with which I had simultaneously to deal. My alibi had given birth to a monster that was turning out to be far more unmanageable than the plight he had been created to deflect attention from.

Once I lost her I tried hard to appreciate the contour of the country, the swell of the bluegreen sea; how, for example, certain small craft rose then collapsed on an excretion of foam whereas others, sleeker, more single-motored in their dedication to pleasure, in a glide imperceptible to the plebeian and naked eye managed to relegate that excretion to their wake—as their wake. Where was the lesson inside this fine distinction and what was the meaning of the momentary exultation, even grandeur, accruing upon the making of such a distinction, fine or not, to wit, that as bad as craft A appeared to be in the flesh in retrospect I had to admit it was nothing like craft B. Could the world of worldlings be classified away according to these two craft types. These two very different crafts were now drifting side by side toward the horizon, the winking sun allowing their rumps to laugh in my face. But they couldn't be laughing—because of the enormous strength devolving upon me directly through the imminence of my connection to the rocks at this very moment rising up to redirect—that is to say, strangle—the perception somewhat more than latent in the receding rumps and conducive to venomous laughter. This newfound strength had become their perception, which now could only express the best in me.

I sighted one of the more imposing specimens in the middle distance—one of the most beautiful though they were all beautiful especially when layered with the luminosity of noon that was always the luminosity of an elsewhere, an elsewhere dreamed of elsewhere. While its bulk still vaguely shimmered I wanted to convey that I was not gazingly soliciting its awareness of my long-awaited arrival on the scene. Having at first a vaguely comforting sense—of outrage—that this rock, zigzagging out of the maze of its fellows, should dare to presume I was observing it closely, hugging its shore, imperceptibly I shunted to a vague and sideline look in its general direction and that out of mere idle curiosity—the idle curiosity springing preponderantly from strength and having its right on one's side to say nothing of a sublime and supreme indifference to all consequences. Yet just as imperceptibly though far more damningly this verificatory look—this shunted side-long stare to determine—but idly, idly, with consummate and magisterial indifference—if my initial close observation was suspected or detected—became the look of throbbing interest that justified whatever suspicions I might have taken it into my head to ascribe to the sun-drink hulk. So I was roped in more intricately to the world of the rocks and its ways, actively sponsoring a relation I had heartily hoped to steer clear of [having returned in all innocence to chuckle over and scrutinize that total absence of relation with which I had believed myself saddled] yet of whose manifestation—fulguration—deflagration—at last some latent symptom—hers, mine, the little ones'—was growing more and more impatient. And this relation was well on the way to reinforcing—this time definitively and without appeal—its incompatibility with all other relations—to the little ones, for example, to the hovel itself, more innocent than the little ones ever could be and just as much in need of a light and loving uncontaminated touch.

Yet each visit—at least as far as I could remember in this pullulating haze—had proceeded in just the same way to the same point of definitive no return. Each visit, just like this one, had seemed—with the very same outraged sidelong look transformed *imperceptibly* into a declaration of irreparable irrevocable enthrallment—an unspeakably final throwing off of the chains of pretense compliments of, at last, definitive capitulation before the fissured craggy psychopomps trained to guide toward and establish me within a hell of unbounded pleasure. Now what was the formula inculcated in grade school for authentic obsession: Number of visits to degradation site divided by coefficient of negligence with respect to godly and familial things. Each time it seemed I was satisfying these formulaic conditions flawlessly. And yet always I came away feeling I had failed with respect not only to the obsession—to degradation and prostration—but to repudiation of the everyday world as well. In the west a lightfooted flotilla, at high noon already suggesting sunset—at any rate, a cooler freer play of light, less humorless than noon's—was massing. It would not be easy assimilating this event to my concept of day. For the massing was less a constituent than a faroff commentary on day's deficiency and its solemn vauntings of underepressible standstill that were, in the long run, so easy to deflate.

I sat down. No goats in sight. I was waiting for the rocks to emerge although they were already before me. There was a certain connection among and between them. But this connection had escaped the cruel and capricious sway of those three weird siblings: conspiracy, camarilla, and cabal. Something in the way rock face answered to rock face—raucously, brutally, each intent on drinking in its own draught of pleasure, while at the same time playfully and not so playfully taunting the unique and momentary vehicle of that pleasure—something in their way set me free of my usually coherent concerns, about her, the little ones, the hovel itself. The thought of a full-time job with a benefit package worthy of Saint Nick was further away than the now receding flotilla. All was far away except rock answering to rock, each face basking in a spare and undulating obliviousness to the puny outrage of delighted onlookers. My eagerness for some kind of release obliterated all others—and time in tandem. Its moment was slow in coming, it was not coming, at least not toward me. They remained, the rock faces, latent in the slight breeze from the sea that froze my innards but revealed how putatively insentient things were able to convert all epiphenomena to the cause of unrelievable heat. There was no way to reach them for they had not yet awakened my body in such a way as to enable me to leave it—and soul—obliterated behind as I made my way toward fusion with and among the fusing shapes. Or so I thought. Looking straight at them I was already remembering the look somewhere in the flesh of their collective eye. They were listening, or rather not so much listening as waiting for me to look up and beyond this or that knotted and herb-infested crevice to their real core of sentiency so as—at the very moment when they knew they had me—to proclaim their absorption in anything but what they or I thought I was doing to distract them. In a word, they were practiced dissimulators. But this dissimulation, impaled on a ray of waning sunlight, was very much in keeping with its charm, now theirs, now more, far more, than their charm, mere charm—their seductive undulation, say, of sheer mass, streaked with the cruelty peculiar to androgynes of a certain ethnic stripe. Yet in the face of that seductiveness—whose mercilessness had nothing—I repeat—nothing to do with the rocks—nothing! nothing!—and everything with the slant of sun rebounded from the surface of a sea flayed by the coniferiform wakes of pleasure craft—in the face of that seductiveness I became convinced of having just lost something, precious of course, some gift presented or extorted in a hallowed moment of domestic reconciliation, earnest of a long life crowded out by the symptoms of little ones, handsel of delicately veined joys yet to come. And feeling I had just lost what could never be identified much less retrieved, even if the measliest of scrimshaw keepsakes, my only recourse was to invoke a long line of losses from what was now an extinct and previous life to narcotize me to this one which for the [present] life of me I could not localize. Is it any wonder then that I wanted to give it all up to the extent not only of not searching for a full-time job but of gingerly putting one foot in front of the other the way I had long before been taught, I forget for what purpose. Yet somehow something, maybe the flight of a gull overhead, propelled me to resumption of the maneuvers of a brute craving to survive unmackled by the recent infliction of I still knew not what.

So it is safe to say that whatever the other effects of affiliation of sun and rocks, and rocks and rocks, and sun and rocks and sun, it had induced a definitive loss—more, far more, than a mere sense of loss—authentic loss but with object still unknown because still in base and retorsive collaboration with the forces propagatory of loss. I felt something near me. My first thought—in the form of a testicular shiver—that it had come in the name of replenishment.

Her. Though there were no goats in sight, probably for miles and miles and miles, she commented, And there are more and more couples of *that* sort. Men and goats, I mean. Goats and men. And worst of all—after their miscegenative incursions among the ravenous ghosts of men—goats and goats. Beautiful goats, she added, with the impatient and emphatic forthrightness of one who wants through utterance, all too fleeting because all too accelerated because all too incongruous with more pervasive beliefs, to consign some unwary other, any old other, to his—her—its—own initial point of intimidatedness no longer desirable because no longer consonant with glorious flight from self to a more unpredictable therefore more glamorous site. But for all her talk would she have been able to witness unappalled my own brawny fusion with a goat on some thorny slope sequestered. No: her global brashness made it all too clear, at least for me, that such implausible couplings were only to be contemplated from afar—as a *divertissement* practicable in a world not quite our own. And some of these beautiful goaties have very flabby stifles, she added. For she had what she took to be very flabby thighs. Yes, she insisted, in the face of a look her continuing uneasiness was obliged to interpret as skeptical—demonically so—skeptical indeed though not, she failed to realize, so much of what she said—what did I care if freethinking goats were flauntingly unstylish enough to pamper very flabby thighs—as of the provenance of, warrant for, such unintelligibly shrill emphasis. In the face of skepticism she became still more emphatic, continuing to take sluggish bafflement for goading disbelief. I took pity—or gave free rein to the signs of pity—stroked her thighs, though not as flabby, alas, as she gave out. But as I stroked, not from instinctive tenderness, nor even instinctive compassion, merely from a frigid sense of what is nomically meet under certain circumstances—she smiled, as at the fatuity of my gesture. It was she who was skeptical now, of my deference, no doubt, become an inconceivable and inconsequential burst of undue alarm, inappropriately striving to enlighten her about a state of soul that did not exist—once, that is, the light of sweet reason was trained upon it. Her state of soul existed as long as it could go on crying out for a consolation cruelly denied it. Once in being, that consolation could only crowd out the state of soul for which it had been rushed in. This state of soul clamoring for consolation and the consolation itself simply *were not of the coexistence variety*. I drove her off.

I felt something near me. My first thought: It was she come back. When whatever it was did not step forward my second thought was that whatever I had lost was about to be restored. I turned away for while it was definitely if vaguely advancing I did not want it to know I was the least bit aware of its encroachment. For I wanted it to bask—or rather I wanted to bask—in its consciousness of my innocence, my indifference, where indemnifying turns of events were concerned. I wanted to become that alien consciousness, to achieve self-transcendence by performing in such a way as to stimulate the subreptions of that consciousness. But after awhile I could no longer control my curiosity and the fever pitch of theatricality dwindled and ultimately oozed into a shameless and overexpectant leering at the imminent form, the soon-to-be-conspicuously-advancing form, to determine whether it suspected or was beginning to dare to suspect that I was aware of it, looking its way, or getting ready to do so, as I had done with so many of the rock faces and with so many other prior objects that had not been rock faces.

Once again a verificatory look outside myself in the service of determining whether a particular form was daring to make any untoward assumptions managed to justify the very assumptions of whose impudent absurdity that look had intended to convince it. The dehortative look aimed at intimidating an absurdity once again ended up vindicating it. I consequently turned away as fast as I had turned toward. It was a goat. The minute I was sure it was a goat—one of hers, in the sense of seeming a plausible goad to her symptom—I galloped away, became myself a goat, hid in a fissure of the first rock face to hand: a very large one, so it turned out, and lavishly clogged with a delicate brushwork of brownish hairs oriented at right angles to the upthrust of the rock itself though from a distance, minuscule, bare, and without apparent organization. It was cozy in my little fissure. Yet the more foolproof the more I was convinced that turning around at any moment I would be confronted with the goat—my galloping goat—and in a stance far more conducive to belittling than I had presented moments before when we were separated by the coarctations of field and stream. A sense of being foolproof and adroit, then, was indistinguishable from frenzied anticipation of the goat's sudden vanquishing encroachment. I was suddenly no more than what the goat, my pursuer the goat, failed to comprehend and was therefore setting out to isolate and destroy. In this cranny of retrospect I could not come to grips with the funeral procession of events: The terrified discovery of loss, her arrival, outraged departure, appearance of the goat with a brazen air of having been frantically importuned for nothing. I could not subsume these events and others—emergence into the shadow of the rocks, vicarious participation in their noonday riot—under the rubric: I. They were always subsuming me first, were always bigger than any explanations available to and stutteringly proffered by that I. I was but an intermittent element within each of these events, which might, in toto, belong to a being at once infinitely bigger and far simpler. Maybe they belonged—in toto or otherwise—to no being—and as an eruption of purest energy come from nowhere and going nowhere had seen fit to bore a hole through me and my stances en route to that nowhere. So that we—goat and rocks and I, she and the hovel and the hairclogged mofettes—merest accidents—might not be completely deluded to hope for ultimate subtilized inclusion into something wider and grander than our miserable past, present, and future.

The goat's encroachment was calling me into question. Delivered up to the rocks I had been suddenly approached as something other than what I thought myself to be, and though I still had only the merest glimpse of what that other was I knew I did not like it and that she and the little ones would not like it—must not like it—if the life of the hovel was to remain intact if not exemplary—told myself I was baffled though who's to say what was stronger or more authentic, bafflement or revulsion, that is, the fascinated revulsion of complete and instantaneous comprehension allowing only for a playing at bafflement. And all through my subsequent divagations I vowed to keep the little ones in mind, far away, judging, abandoned, judging because abandoned, or rather it was their abandonment that took over and impeached, prosecuted, condemned for life and beyond, since they themselves were still incapable of assessing this my monumental unworthiness for the title of father. Who and what was I for my pursuer, for myself mirrored in the oblated depths of my pursuer, he who, I flattered myself, was fast turning out to be my pursuer, indefatigable with a singlemindedness commensurate with my newly-discovered own. Yet so suspended at the end of his leash what could I hope to be for, toward, the little ones.

I looked toward the few trees in the distance for an answer. I assumed they were growing according to divine plan. But what little wind there was to go around—once again, according to the divine plan—was being pompously and ponderously bandied about by the uppermost boughs and as this unconvincing form of distributional deliberation had already been going on far too long for my taste and gave every indication of continuing to do so and to hell with my taste or lack of same, when the now puny ration was at last approved for release and descended for ostensible allocation among the lower orders of twigs, twiglets, petioles, nodes, and scraps of node, there was of course no longer any wind to speak of, only the scrappiest memory of its grit and fetor.

I had to get back to the rocks. As if after a day of storm afflicting not only the rocks but their irregular spurts of crabgrass and the sands below and the sea and the sky and the unsmoking hovels dotting the skyline, a serrated edge of sunpatches advancing, sent out veritable antennae of reconciliation, struggled to make amends. The little army encouraged me to think of the rocks and what must constitute my particular connection to their mottled faces. But all of a sudden something in the connection or in the ultimacy of a nonconnection decked out with all the gewgaws of a connection made it as absurd to think of the connection as to mistake the sun patches, tenaciously proceeding, though gingerly, toward the massive trunks of distant trees—still defective in their windy deliberations—or toward their not quite massive five-o-clock shadows, for a permanent part of the increasingly assarted terrain. But I could not quite decide what in particular all mixed up in my craving—hunger—desire—for the rocks justified its— the craving's—comparison to this venial mistake of a too fanciful tourist entranced by sunspots advancing and bole shadows retrenching. So I sighed, audibly, relieved that for once the little ones were not present to witness what they could construe only as the grotesqueness of my too ghastly and un-self-conscious comfort amid the ruins of the landscape. For it was a landscape. Just because I was amidst those ruins did not mean I had already contaminated them with my nonbeing. For even if my most preponderant feeling at this juncture pointed to—even if every single quale however fleeting and remote bodied forth—a profound and tortured discomfort, in relation to the little, blessedly absent, ones my very discomfort of squirming and squawking could only be undergone as easeful complacency bordering on the smug and branding me irrevocably—once again from the point of view of these same little ones not yet acceded to, herniated into, being and therefore in spite of themselves exemplarily fastidious—as one of that being's arch-myrmidons grotesquely, smugly, irrevocably entrenched in its slime. Far from accepting as natural the ways of being they had yet to undergo the inevitably gradual, reluctant, unknowing acceptation of chauvinistic entrenchment in a home slime in whose propagation, come to think of it, already each had a preeminent stake.

And so I must embody a world—a landscape—an iniquity of rock faces—to which they did not yet belong and to which they could not even conceive of themselves belonging. Yes, yes, yes, from their point of view I was very much in being, a seasoned denizen of the landscape, and for all my tergiversation between relation and nonrelation to the rocks, not unlike those artist folk she, their universal mother, was forever denouncing, for my edification and always with a broomstick or vacuum cleaner in her arms and perhaps rightly, as positively superfetatory in their misguidedness for with all their ranting and raving over an unbearable estrangement when all was ranted and raved wasn't the lamentation and jobation over said estrangement in actual fact the impregnable schema of an entrenchment any butcher or word processor might envy. She had always urged me against any untoward transumptions of such a program since it could hardly apply to a peasant, at once impish and oafish, like me. So here I was, on the verge of discovering that this, my unspoken stance of estrangement, was perhaps the most insufferably complacent form of entrenchedness in being known to fish or fowl. And in spite of all her dehortations against following in the footsteps of these artist folk I fancied myself one for I was beginning to see the rock faces and the absent little ones recoiling from their seeing me as smugly—insufferably—one with the landscape and the goats and the hovel and even her, its heart and soul,—I was beginning to see them—it—all differently, as through a telefoto lens of wizened pathos. And this was not at all the way of my seeing in the past, so much the way of others, many many many others.

To shake myself free of entrenchment in rocky terrain, which I had all along been in danger of mistaking for an authentic relation to the rocks themselves, once I sensed the goat was gone I stepped aside in such a way as to thwart and undo any residual concretization of that relation. The rocks could only lead me to a bad end beyond that bad end to which I was already betrothed. I tried to move off as I seemed to remember the goat moving, that is, with a certain forceful thrust of the instep yoked to a careful waddling separation of the plenteous thighs as if in alleviation of an excruciatingly painful hemorrhoid for which, as everybody knows, the only authentic balsam is the plectral wind of an odorless fart strafing the site of inflammation. Such a gait promised, though precisely where and by whom? not only to bypass and elude whatever remained of my craving for a relation to the rocks but, more important, to transform me into a creature—if a creature was what I wished to become—totally new, totally *other*, much more forthright, manly, and dependably exempt from the little subterfuges of villainy I regret to admit I had practiced and on more than one occasion. Though I must confess I did not relish the thought of being forthright, manly, and subterfugeless all at the same time. I had been flattering myself that I was forever on the verge of gliding into a relation with the rocks whereas without knowing what I had all along been seeking was authentic collision—with some object or, better yet, incident as object, able by allowing me to extricate myself from its mangled browse to enhance my self-esteem, that is, construct myself anew, that is, from scratch while simultaneously hallucinating through newfound hand, foot, and a host of other newfound body parts a sodality with my fellows so wide-ranging and intense as to eliminate any subsequent search for rocky refuges and hair-clogged havens.

I noted another clump of scrubby trees on the far side of a small ravine, sister to this in which I had just lost her. As collision mates, playing ratchet wheel to my tappet, maybe these would do, especially since they closely resembled guinea fowl primping and preening against the wind. But as I stared at them, expecting that at any moment the goat—my goat—might emerge from between their ravaged bulbous trunks, I was forced over and over and over again to revise my initial conception of the logic of their unfolding: that is, three squat followed by one slightly less so, and so on, and so forth. In actual fact, it was two squat, followed by two not so squat, followed by three even less squat than most, followed once again by two squat, and so on, and so forth. I got closer and closer but why bother trying to collide rehabilitatingly with forms whose logic I could not unravel. As I advanced, whether on the trees or on the rock faces once more I could not say, he, suddenly appearing, advanced also. I did not know to what I might attribute first the reappearance then the advancing toward except his being after all in her service, as guardian of the unfathered little ones, and for whose tutelage and tuition all concerned were simply too too grateful as being everywhere consonant with standards only I could claim to find too exalted. I did not know where I was going, whether to trees or rocks. But it did not matter, every movement away or toward one or the other, away or toward one or the other, was now constitutive of a language elaborated for the benefit of the goat—every movement toward or away was now a clue among clues thanks to which he could later explain what this all meant—all this going toward the rocks in the absence of concrete relation. But he was growing irritable, I could tell, for he scratched his anus with a hindpaw, which signified in fact less irritability than irritation repressed in a grand show of therapeutic tact—as if my going toward the rocks or away from the trees had somehow been an undamped and blatant expression of grandiose self-conception indulged at her expense and, worse, at the expense of the little ones. He had very little patience, then, what with his right hindpaw scratching the lining of his anus and his left front dewclaw grazing his underdeveloped right tit, for what my going toward the rocks, if we may finally refer to it as that, in his view dangerously suggested to my own mind of a special status, a destiny too complex for comparison to that of the run of beings. Every movement toward, for me fraught with tormenting dangers, struck *him* as nothing more nor less than a dandified criminal neglect of the little ones.

At the same time I could not help thinking this dour impatience with my outbursts of movement toward and away from the rocks had little enough to do with me, had much more—had everything—to do with all the other movers toward and away from—rocks or maidenhair ferns or the sea itself—with whom he was wont or obliged professionally to collide. When he was out of sight I could not move. I mean, there was nothing to do, no going back to her and to the little ones, much less in the general direction of the rocks. Everything was suspended until his return. Everything was suspended until he could explain—his dourness and how much of it had been prompted by my unseemly advertisement of exultation consequent to secret sweltering anticipation of a relation to the rocks at last and how much based on the fatigue of disgust at having to contend, day in and day out, with a long line of similarly fateful sufferers, excruciatingly tedious to observe yet as strangely insusceptible to patternizing as the long line of trees into which he had just been reabsorbed.

Should I go on, I asked myself, once he was gone and the landscape began receding toward night. At the same time I marveled at myself already going on, and more than merely going on, moving swiftly in the direction of the hut, toward her, presumably, and the little ones. Was this moving swiftly in brute defiance of him, goat of goats, or was it simply a case of his apparent abandonment ultimately making things easier? On I went, into shadow. In fact I was still living toward our next encounter: Back in the hovel I was once again overcome with disgust at the state of things, at the little ones bawling, the stickiness of surfaces undone. All was ooze and rejectamenta. Moving into a corner I put a sheet over my head to fall asleep as quickly as possible. I awoke to find myself soaked with urine, no one's but my own. Such lack of control stabbed me to the heart. Knowing I would be unable to fall asleep again I set about washing what little there was of my bedclothes, screamed, shook her till she was black and blue, tried in the midst of all my transports to smile at the little ones, stamped my foot until the snot came popping right out of my nose.

As she naturally turned away in disgust I even more naturally feared—and raged—that she might end up choosing to love no longer what, barring my engagement with the rocks, must be my purest part: my transports—of rage, of incontinence, of snotpopping. I'm not strong enough, she said, guessing my thoughts and looking round the tiny yurt serving as agora, peristyle, bedroom, kitchen, gentleman's study, loo, imperial dining room, orlop, oubliette, pergola, haha, paddock, solarium, and, needless to say, shrine of our unextinguishable passion—its last relic and halidom, its nether-tending naos, cella, adytum—which look round and back served pathetically—almost cinematically—to suggest she might have been, strong enough that is, if only we hadn't been saddled and over so minuscule an interval with so many little ones and the far more than suboptimal straits to which their seemingly endless proliferation had managed to reduce us. This meant she must ask me to leave. For a split second I was terrified even if I knew this dismissal would allow me to legitimately pursue the rocks in all their unburnished glory. But anger ultimately carried the day—anger at what her limpid little response betrayed of limits to what should have been a boundless devotion to a boundless discontent, supplemented by the residue of whatever centuries before had given rise to the tantrum that had, in turn, provoked the limpid little response—and thereby anesthetized me to any sorrow in the face of jettison.

So you want me out, I suggested. She looked stricken: Her terror reassured me, though my suggestion was suddenly alive with so many hidden clauses it was impossible to pinpoint the precise target of her terror. If I was presenting my most extreme formulation in order to have it refuted it was nevertheless mixed up with so many other imputations there would be no reassuring myself definitively no matter what her response. I wanted her to refute my extremest formulation and at the same time punish her for compelling my recourse to it. I saw you, she said, among the rocks. I felt sorry, those strange strange rocks. This was clearly praise for me—brave enough and henotheistic enough and man-of-the-people enough to venture out alone among those embrowned and derelict forms craved by nobody respectable yet no less desirable for all that. Then she gasped and howled so loudly the little ones were obliged to flee in terror. This access of terror made the rocks so temporarily strange to my mind's eye that I ended up incapable of understanding how I ever could have considered consorting with such beings. Then she turned away and for the split second of the turning— without gasps, without howls—I admired her as I would have admired any storyteller who manages to begin or end his story before either way it can accede—metastasize—to meaning, to what the slobbering scholiasts take for meaning. Afraid her slur might have destroyed them for good, I went away in search of the only being who could define my relation to the rocks. The goat did not come.

I noted one rock face rising high above the others; its crest excited me. I hurried toward it as if for dear life but in stumbling caught—or rather had visited upon my throbbing sightlessness—an oversized glimpse of everything just below yet indissolubly bound to the crest and everything below was so uncrestlike, so sluggish and ordinary, so rooted in the overtness of everyday cravings, that I could only feel enormous relief at having been saved—and in the nick of time—from incision by a glaring overpowering mystery that had only seemed autonomously beyond connection and collusion with the brute manifestations of survival at any cost. Pleased with a narrow escape which I now figured as redounding completely to the credit of my own ingenuity, I thought of going on, with or without the goat's assistance, to all the other rock faces and by getting a definite hold on them in the same brashly adroit manner manage to have done with them at last and be never again obliged to pursue and give up my life to them.

I came now upon a pair, not a single rock, but a wedded pair. In the winking sunlight one seemed to be guffawing at what the other had just said. But already the first had that forward-looking blunted repudiating look of one who lest he be taken to task by the pursuing gaze of its target wants at all cost to be dissociated from whatever he may have been compelled to utter at some moment in the now very uninteresting and for all practical purposes remote past. Maybe I was the target though my gaze was not reproachfully in their wake but right in front of them and devoid of reproach, of meaning even. Now that the second rock face was the perduring repository of the stale winking remark—something to do with my mode of dress or mode of living with her and the little ones deducible from my dress—it had to be gotten rid of, was superfluous. At any rate, this joker was exalted through having been able to squander what another was obliged to treasure which treasure was now yapping uncomfortably at his, the joker's, royal rear end. All of sudden the schism was terminated: They were laughing at me, I looked around, nobody else in sight. But they couldn't be laughing at me because of the golden and miraculous sense of purpose that had just supervened through my discovery of yet another rock face. Clearly I had never given up the idea of a strolling and exhaustive inventory effecting their annihilation in behalf of health. In my advance—which was also a definitive repudiation of the grinning dyad—I felt I must be elaborating a text worthy of the goat's—my goat's—most ingenious decipherment. The supervening strength in arms, legs, groin, and dew-claws had uprisen to redirect—strangle—their erroneous perception. Or rather, their—the dyad's—misperception was now indistinguishable from my strength, was my strength, was a tiny little flaw at the heart of that strength, a strength so towering and indefatigable it no longer sought his—anybody's decipherment. In short, I was on the verge of that singular illumination that precedes a rainstorm. NO. What is the name of the rhetorical figure totally, revelingly, flauntingly inappropriate to a situation at hand and the sole purpose of whose imposition is to displace—to oust—some more correct rival. Illumination or no illumination, as if to crown this marvel of a newfound freedom in moving easily among the rocks, among my cravings for the rocks, without the slightest foreboding that these craving movements and moving cravings were in any way mediatized by the whims of a larger appetite—for scrutiny, diagnosis, pigeonholing—I discovered I was no longer smitten, was left totally cold. And I wasn't just playing as sometimes I did at being left totally cold, in the hope that whatever alien consciousness happened to be loitering nearby would, witnessing, be deceived sufficiently to justify my perception of its perception of my self as very much a sterling perception and of a self magisterially uninhabited and uninhabitable by such dregs as my own dissimulated true cravings: So powerful is another's consciousness as a momentary filler—usurper—of our own. Not that I always wanted to be filled: Sometimes I wanted to strangle the alien consciousness—all alien consciousnesses. No, this time I was authentically indifferent to the rocks and no stronger proof than my entrancement—no other word will do—once again by trees, but this time holding out no tempting prospect of an impregnable logic somewhere resident in the ways and means of their deployment.

Though I took to them not only at once but passionately I was at every moment, with equal passionateness, assailed by the question: How passionately in fact have I taken to them. I turned away to consider the matter, walked on, and whenever their image assailed I was happy. They were now the cipher of a private store, a private haunting. Or were they—stumped and bowled over and in the last paroxysm or trance of leafless misery—mere bits and pieces of an exurban decor annexed for my own self-aggrandizement. But somewhere there had to be true feeling, somewhere I had to be deeply moved, authentically moved, no. For *authentically moved* and asthenic specimens like it were mere puffery for my innate goodness. Authentically threatened, then. And yet as I moved further and further away from their site—to test the grain, the resiliency, of the connection—the discrete instances—upsurges—of their recurrence stank of self-induced vomiting. I turned quickly in their direction, caught sight of a goat—the goat—gamboling off in their shadow. This gamboling suggested, told me straight off, that there was an underlying mechanism arranging for these recurrences and that mechanism lubricated by authentic though not very pretty spurts of emotion denuded of any self-mastery or control and very much mixed up with intimations that I was after all not very different from these stumpy forms, bowled over, maimed, and mendicant, and without the courage to look their patron in the eye. I went back to the trees: There were just a few of them, sparsely growing out of cleft unencumbered by grainy beckoning rock faces. Jaundiced leaves did sprout from time to time along the splayed boughs, the horizontal and fortuitous excrescence of their arrowlet-like stems as if alighted for the sole purpose of parasitizing in the manner of the most exotic NO in the manner of mere semi-exotic avifauna every available inch of free surface not impropriated alas in time by native and intrinsic outgrowths. I wondered if seeing such thoughts, thinking such sights, was taking me as far from the rocks and, more important, the being I became delivered up to the craving they provoked, as I professed to be. For these trees—I saw it now—were most atypical, too atypical to sustain the contemplation of their marginality as an antidote to my craving for the rocks. These then were not to be considered dragomen within a whole new domain proudly counterpoiseworthy to that of the rocks but merely an incarnated transition to still another one of their eruptions.

Buoyed up neither by trees nor by my goat I observed her advancing, coming toward me, so to speak, on wings of reprobation as fleet it would appear as in those golden days when without the little ones to obstruct the progress of an infatuation vaster than summer evening sunsets we were a-courting. She suggested—I could not hear because of the surf. At first I thought she was proposing I move back even if now I had no definite recollection of having moved out. But all she was suggesting, as it turned out, was a little walk among the rocks without the children. I broke into a cold sweat, I was not ready for such an offer even if there had been when stalking the rock faces many a moment when I had dreamed of it. In stroking this or that ventifact, lapillus, magma chip, hadn't I in fact been stroking her gaminlike breasts, the curve of her chin giving forth an odor of privet. I know it's difficult, she said, at this point. Was she up-to-date regarding the crisis of the trees on whose naked boughs their very own foliage had come to alight horizontal, voracious, and alien as birds of prey? It *is*, I said. She looked at me with outrage tinged with disbelief and relief. Until a minute before she had wished to incarnate no more outrage and disgust tinged with the relish of disbelief than could be assimilated to the archetype of loving little woman bravely fronting the home front. And I had complied, steering hygienically clear of her as a shrew of a particular type whose barbs were keenly directed toward the noisome particularity in me. Instead I redirected them innocuously toward my archetype, the difficult but loving breadwinner. Now she was through wanting to generate no more malice than was assimilable to her archetype; she craved my

gut. It was all right for her to say *it* was difficult, whatever it was—
proposed idyll or suburban death with dignity; I, however, was expected
to refute this difficulty with all the boyish apologizing zeal at my
disposal. She had needed to believe I would be serious enough in my
intentions of our walking over the rock faces to allow her to refrain in
seemly fashion and with impeccable dignity from having to nurture,
that is to say, goad, those intentions into unequivocating action. So that
now more than ever—with me hemming and hawing—she wanted such
a walk. Still she wanted it less than she didn't want it. What's the point,
she murmured finally, as if tactfully pinpointing the absurdity at the
heart of this my childish spontaneity sweeping everything before it.
We'll walk around, get lost, remember too late the little ones have to be
fed and put to sleep. I was not sure whether she was belittling the
invitation, which now seemed to have originated with me, or my reluctance to honor that invitation, whatever its provenance. By belittling
the occasion that was not to be was she masking genuine disappointment or simply plausibilizing her way out of what was supremely
distasteful now that I was electioneering for it. But how was she able to
transmute my revolted quietism into a form of electioneering?

　　　She moved off. I don't know where she was going but the
minute she was out of sight the goat emerged from the cluster of stumps.
I turned away, for I had nothing to offer, certainly no craving for the
rocks, was therefore wasting his time with my trivial concerns, the
bloated demands of my insignificance were standing in the way of his
far more significant pursuit of well-being, professional or other. Surely
there must be a mother goat and little ones to whom he, unlike me, was
vociferously and unambiguously attached. So how dare I stand in the
way of that well-being hungering—I could see it in his deepset eyes—to
play itself out on the great stage of the world. At the same time from the
way he persisted in circling me he appeared to be more than a little
intrigued by my insignificance, or rather NO or rather NO or rather, by
my conception—doubtless palpable, even undulatory, in every gesture—of that insignificance. After all, how dare I believe my being was
subsidiary to anybody else's. I stepped forward emboldened, toward the
rocks but not with the rocks in mind, the movement liberating the
discovery that this conviction of venal exploitation through the machi-

nations of a lack of authentic and significant torment of one—and therefore all and sundry—laboring against authentic odds in behalf of the realization of authentic hopes was in actual fact the core of my torment and a very real, authentic, and significant torment it was, and very much in need of decipherment. Anyone holding fast to such a conviction was clearly tormented beyond the imputation of a vile deception perpetrated on unwitting betters. Yet finding myself once more among the rocks, among those most lavishly and vigorously riddled with hair-clogged fissures, I was again overwhelmed with self-reproach for daring to drain the goat's capacity for being due, it was true, to my mewling insignificance but all of a sudden and no less significantly to this well-nigh overwhelming sense of significance, undeserved and sucked bloated from a proscribed sphere, that of the rocks. Suddenly overwhelmed with potency in that sphere, though of what the potency consisted I hadn't the faintest idea, I was understandably compelled to take pity on those, like him, meagerly consigned to wanting to flourish only in this. What if the potency was nothing but the hallucinogenic arrogance peculiar to that sector of the population that considers itself superior to all vulgarity of conspicuous effort and even more conspicuous finished product? Having managed never to prolapse their grandiose claims into the terrain of specificity they are able to entertain to their dying day and well beyond the sense of an achievement in comparison with which all palpably finished works stink promptly and contemptibly of scrimshaw. I turned my foot in such a way as to underline my awareness that it was her business to be hounding me, downward and downward, and thereby deflate my arrogance if arrogance was indeed the pith and marrow of this potency without bound. But from a certain recoiling movement, almost pietistic, in return, I gathered the creature—I've taken to calling him the creature—was more estranged and outraged by my ironic detachment in the face of her persecutions than by the persecutions themselves. Clearly he could not imagine a man being denigratingly dissatisfied with women and, by extension, with little ones. I was stomping on sacred ground.

Lying down on the flattened face of a rock, I took to caressing its contours and calling out, Cacabelle, Cacabelle Jenkins, all the time pointing in the general direction of our hut. And then, simply because at that very moment a bole chose to emerge from shadow and be flayed by the shadow of boughs overhanging I changed my devilish cry to: Chelsea, Chelsea O'Butterworth, or Chelsea O'Butterheinie, I don't remember which. For there were, when all was said and done, so many new names at our disposal and each a clean slate delivering us up, she and I, but always in the goat's vicinity, to a new, a better, life, a life beyond rocks and goats and indebted to neither's *agence provocatrice*. Each new name, I tried to explain, by looking languidly westward toward where the sunset should have been, was a way of wishing her away, rather, a certain aspect of her, or of our life together, or those foulsmelling private parts brought to birth by corresponding parts in her. But he did not rise to the bait of my eloquence, remained dour and on the lookout.

Purposely turning east he kicked dry earth back in my direction. This had to mean that as far as he was concerned each naming induced an outflow of incompatible overtones—each subsuming a certain underappreciated facet of her being—forced basely to cohabit with the name of the moment as leading tone. His shortlived glance skyward added, So many incompossibles forced to commingle in the stagnant pool of the name, degrading to bearer and deviser. And worse: Each naming is an exercise in suppression—of both you and her—a cutting off at the incandescent root of so many of her radiant qualities and of all possible approach to a delight in such qualities. So, according to him I had lost her forever. But I couldn't permit myself the luxury of a way in to that sense of loss since I did not have at my fingertips, to dampen its excruciation through the process of verification, some indefatigable algorithm capable of engendering through lack of closedness a frustration so vast there would not possibly be any time for lamenting the loss itself.

He strutted off, with an uncharacteristic heaviness in the haunches. The rocks, at his approach, rose up as they never had, never would, for me. Unlike me he did not need—his haunches said as much—to be linked in bridling rage to some torturer in whose shadow only was it permissible to run out toward impossible communion with the unmentionable. Unlike me he did not need a torturer in whose shadow—the merest shadow of an impregnable foothold—he was allowed to pursue the unspeakable crevices which pursuit would of course have to be presented to himself—if he were I—as defiant emancipation from said torturer's domination—desperately if sourly craved.

Yet I was and still am highly suspicious of this sharp—this too sharp—contrast—this almost blindingly glaring contrast—between his relation to the rocks and mine: Stinks too much of the kind of mock meaning too much mistaken for meaning by our little cowpokes and sciolists. How could—can—I even think of speaking of his relation to the rocks. Not that I wouldn't under other circumstances be tickled absolutely pink to find myself speaking of that preponderating relation to the rocks even if it meant pulling them right out from under mine for that would also mean an end to the rocks, as far as I was concerned, as well as an end to the goat, to her, to the little ones, to me. At any rate, suspicions or no, there he was: grazing among them, the biggest and most undulatingly fissured of the rock faces, and pulling them to pieces as if they were so many blades of crabgrass duly apportioned to the scythe that was he. But at the same time it was unclear—blessed unclarity—even at the moment when I had his scythelike doings before my eyes—that this was a cut-and-dried case of blatant and unforeseen poaching on the part of some little camarilla of one slobberingly consecrated to toppling the possibility of any pleasure-taking among my very own preserves. More and more and more it was coming to have, this ambling of my goat among my rocks, the characteristic resonance of a self-inflicted rent deep in the brain tissue of happiness, of a fruit of my own labors, of my very own little camarilla of one. Yes, yes, yes, I had somehow managed to direct goat to rocks or rocks to goat so as to cover over and ablate the all-too-naked prospect of indivisible ecstasy—the infinite perspective of an impossible happiness. And now I was consecrated not to widening the prospect of that happiness but to somehow righting the self-induced rent, fixing the fissure I myself had induced in a landscape that had all along been ready to welcome me with the openest of arms.

And yet though I had managed, through the agency of the goat—my goat—to destroy my happiness, my impossible ecstasy, because it was simply too frighteningly enormous when compared to the drudgery to which I was used, still I found myself reacting to the turn events had taken as if that turn had not been taken as all—as if, in other words, two mutually exclusive possibilities, my infinite perspective of an impossible happiness terrifyingly drenched in the choicest secretions of the rocks AND the goat's—still my goat's—retorsive usurpation of that happiness compliments of my own clumsy lack of foresight or excess of same were unfolding simultaneously thereby afflicting me with the inconveniences—closer to incurable afflictions—specific to each. So that I did not even have the option of curing myself of belief in the prospect of happiness through moxibustive substitution of the old goat amid its grassy surfaces. On the one hand he had usurped my place among the rocks. On the other I was still glued to the prospect held out by that place of a possible, therefore impossible, ecstasy.

Though I had managed, compliments of the goat, to destroy all possibility of happiness now and forever I was reacting as if that possibility was still very much a real one, that is to say, very much an encumbrance in the way of choosing a definitive course of active inter-vention that could rid me at last of all goat-occasioned unhappiness. I was enjoying both the fruits of unhappiness and all the messy obstruc-tions to its undoing occasioned by encroachment of its too viscous opposite. I badly needed to get over this interval of ecstasy—of rap-ture—in order to begin planning how to contend with an unhappiness whose exacerbation was directly traceable to the enfeeblement induced by that ecstasy—by that rapture.

I cursed him cavorting on my private property, running his hocks along the hairy fissures, raising the sentient clefts to a pitch of excitement inducible only by someone or something leeringly at ease in administering the frictive caresses of pastern and dewclaw.

I had made it my business to circumscribe all movement—all language as movement—to the vicinity of the rocks so that he, goat that he was, would have something to play with or against, I mean, analyze and diagnose away for all eternity. I had concocted a craving for the rocks to feed his professional self-esteem and sense of purpose. And now he had become addicted to the fuel, was walking off with it between his teeth or between his legs. He had donned the ragged raiment of my craving which, on his scrawny frame, unrecognizably bore none of the telltale stains of shame and despair. He was at home among the rocks, no longer mere rocks but smiling faces clogged with inviting fissures, smooth extensions of sunbaked flesh, undulations poignant with unaccountable tension. So at home that in the distance I could see her smiling and waving, as if cheering him on. And wait a minute, there were the little ones also, smiling and waving or, if not smiling and waving, then certainly given up to a foggy sense that something momentous was taking place, something worthy at last of admiration, even awe. For there he was, taking to the rocks like the proverbial fish to frying pan and into the fire, and continuing to insinuate himself even more deeply—if that was possible—among them. But I should not have been surprised and I was not, no, not the least bit, for this ease, this elasticity of affinity and appeal, came easily from having no fixed beliefs, nothing but the balloon-light baggage of an ever-ready dourness to spray over the tentative and burgeoning beliefs of others: poor folk, like me. This elasticity, vastly appealing, it would appear, to the fissures—look, they were unclogging themselves for his delectation—was what came of maintaining a fructive disequilibrium with halfwit others like me and making sure they never gave way to repose in their own imbalance.

What was particularly enraging was how being drawn to the rocks—and they to him—he managed to dispense with that long apprenticeship to impossible feints, recoils, leaps, and revulsions that had already eaten up so many of my best decades. Assuming that initially I had been driven to the rocks by fear—fear of her, of others too much or too little like her—that fear, ostensibly simple, had long since become festooned with too many of the accessories particular to and constitutive of itself and itself alone—too many of the accessories redolent of a connoisseuring taste gone mad—to be reductible to that initial clinical situation long since irrelevant—unresonant—extinct—to the blind mind's eye of impossible desire. So now that he had taken over—without impossible feints, recoils, leaps, and revulsions—there was no going back, to her, to the little ones, nor forward, for that matter: The rocks clearly preferred him to me. There was of course the sea and all that image summoned forth of a hurling oneself headlong, a being dashed to pieces among the slimy tentacles ravenous below.

I tried hard not to curse him, my friend, the goat, as I watched him—and even when I was no longer watching him—make his way among the too avid forms. He was now very far out at the edge of a precipice, which caused her and the still waving little ones no end of panicked delight. It looked as if, with withers and crop askew, he was conversing and carousing with one of the most upthrusted members of an already highly upthrusted group. I waited, struggling to make music out of what I saw or thought I saw. I tried to transmogrify something fitfully seen into something uninterruptedly heard. But I was completely incapable of coming up with even the tritest ditty much less a plainsong, against which to titrate my rage and detoxified amid the attar of fellow feeling. I could produce no strain in response to the strain of seeing him go on and on and on and out of which he might be depended upon to emerge shorn of his successes, both more and less than a goat, or just a goat, a mere goat, my brother. He was still a loathsome and detestable pig. But it was becoming hard work to go on loathing him unremittingly. He was simply going from rock to rock. Simply he was going from rock to rock. But it was not nor would it ever be a simple going. What, after all, is any act but the hallucinations to which it gives rise. And one such hallucination in this case was the absolute conviction that by going from rock to rock to rock and back again and then forward he was emphasizing my need to relinquish all aspiration in the same sphere. Yet where else did my future lie but among the rocks.

He was not simply betraying our relation—whatever else incontrovertibly founded on my belief in his respect for my craving for the rocks and for ultimate collision with my fate among their fissures—he was appropriating the future. Such a telling—that I must instantaneously relinquish all aspiration in the same—in his—sphere became—with the same instantaneousness—the single voice of the future. I was fixed and frozen at this point in his telling—which was not, I vainly told myself, a telling but a mere going—from rock to rock to rock and back again and then forward and then back and then forward to rock from rock to rock—and could not envision a going beyond it. How his sleek betrayal of our relation in the present had become and for all eternity the voice of the future—my future—its snakelike core of irrefutable prophecy—this I could not determine. All I knew was that this point— this leap—this monstrous transmogrification in place of one thing into another thing—was not worth, in other words, did not bear, in other words, could not bear, thinking about. All I knew was that this quantum leap across the rent—rhegma—raphe in relation to which present betrayal was present betrayal no more but fixed and freezing voice of all eternity pointed to where *somebody* lay bleeding, where *somebody's* pathology was anybody's for the taking. This unlocalizable demarcation—rent—raphe—fissure—cleft—rhegma—seam—this imperceptible leaplike transition whereby a betrayal—a stinking shabby stinging betrayal—became the eternal depiction of the future—all conceivable futures—was the core of the lesion that was I, the shift was my sickness. And only he could cure me.

I looked back: He was still going on, from rock to rock to rock and backwards and forwards, partaking of the humps and hollows and of the even more tantalizingly ambiguous structures in between, without feeling it necessary to give himself up to obstructed moans of self-loathing. He moved slowly, slowly, slowly over a terrain that had just repudiated me, so that I always had more than enough time to transfer my always accessible store of freefloating self-loathing from him to this or that member of his ever-growing seraglio. From the way in which his now bloated loin chose to strike up a conversation with this or that purplish outcropping I was able hastily but surefootedly to evolve a specific rock or rock face trait worthy of revulsion: covetousness, for example, was deducible from a particular specimen's undisguised longing for his tail, or was it his thurl; or worse, far worse, smugness, derived from some other's turning away from me to give itself to the new beloved's waxen barrel—which turning away in the especial way it sustained its turning away suggested an unwavering belief that if things were what they were then there was nothing more sacrosanct than things as they were. Yet two seconds later, though on what seemed like the following day, when he was deep in converse or crural embranglement or both with still another outcropping that outcropping's all-pervasive trait, namely whining righteousness, became the target of my repugnance née self-loathing. And in this way, following him from rock face to rock face, I was able to run the gamut of defects within as an excursion without. In the long run preoccupation with his paramours did little to distract me from the bones I had yet to pick with him. For what was this movement from rock to rock to rock, from cluttered outcropping to cluttered outcropping and back again, but a swelling and extended sermon contrived for my benefit and fanatically urging through each and every labyrinthine period as well as between a decentering—a displacement—of my emphasis from direct endeavor, egocentric thrust of enterprise, to actlets marginal and ancillary. Perhaps I could sponsor some other and thereby become well known to the rocks [thereby provoking their reciprocal craving] trailing that other's clouds of glory and curing myself, even definitively, of my delusions of grandeur and flagitious lack of deference to my betters in the process. Judging from his sermon, then, I was nothing more than another rock— and although from the point of view of this my story I should have been grateful for the hint of such a transformation utilizing only its rawest and most basic elements—from the point of view of my own point of view I was scabrous with disgust and disappointment.

Although I had managed to leap—so what if pathologically— from a sense of his betrayal of our present relation to one of eternal prophecy of future failure unremitting, he could not leap—his footsteps, fettered by his compulsion to obscenely stroke the exposed sunless clefts with a ravenous hoof, bore this out—from my present squalor to a sense that all might change in a moment. Simply because I had no rock-faced champions to plead my interests. According to him, the absence of champions would persist for all time. Unlike me he did not view the stark void in which I stalked unseen as a brazen advertisement of the impossible disjunction between what I was and what the world— for now distilled to the dimensions of his own dyspepsia—took me to be which disjunction was the impossible sign of its momentary and momentous transformation. He failed to perceive that an abjection so raw had no choice but to be with the sign reversed its own imminent exaltation. He took me too literally, or rather from rock to rock to rock and back again and then forward—the endless sermon of his vagrancy.

My interpretation of his wandering among the rocks had no effect whatsoever on that wandering, on his relation to me. In contradistinction to mine, his was not a lethal diversion designed to dissipate anxiety which diversion ultimately became more of a weight around one's colloped neck than the wretched state of affairs initially crying out for cataplasm. Never did he—or so it seemed from his maddeningly leisurely canter—feel the need to give himself up to the rocks as quickly as possible so as to rid himself—via the infernal logic of a misguided metonymy—of the cravings they induced—and so he was never to be found waiting, as I could, for the moment in which he might or might not once and for all succumb or refuse the temptation of the pulsating fissures tongued with overheated hairs to pass and its tide recede on a wasteland of novelty. He took diversion for what it was and no more. It was not as if he had any greater ability than I to suffer ambiguity. He did not suffer ambiguity, he simply bypassed it. Whereas I tended to take the ambiguity—of whether or not I would succumb, whether or not I wanted to succumb, whether or not I was now succumbing at the moment of maximum or most tenuous craving—as a punishment perpetrated for having succumbed once again—to the supremely idiotic and infantile luxury of being what I was, that is, once again striving to become what I already was. If only during those moments when exasperation and disgust and rage and revulsion and lustful anxiety had seemed the only conceivable response to a total absence of stimulus I had somehow managed to be other—other, that is, than that other straitjacketed by the exasperation of so putatively well-meaning but always so rabidly disappointed a parent as he had become, constructing my other before my very eyes and, worse, before the eyes of the unseeing rocks, as a concertedly, laboriously, and deviously concocted attack on his dwindling stock of what was at best an exiguity of well-being.

From the point of view of the story that story would have been stronger if in bold contradistinction to me he had ended up learning to live with, rather than bypass, ambiguity. In short: What is the name of that rhetorical device through which we pretend to summarize clarifyingly but in a manner that has absolutely nothing to do with what came before?—In short, I envied him, wandering up and down, up rock and down, completely surrendered to the ecstasy that only rock faces broiling in the midday sun can give, though their exquisite if slightly less than expert gyrations beneath a full or new-gibbous moon are not to be sneezed at either. He moved off, I remained, maimed by the vision of his expertise in handling not only every species of rock face known to man but their every conceivable collocation in twosomes, threesomes, n-somes, to say nothing of every situation that might arise from such collocations, or worse, fail to arise. Whether or not she decided to take me back and whether or not he was dourly turning his back for good on my craving by making it inimitably his own, thanks to his example I felt stronger, heavier, more able to carry my own weight in being. For his too prominent and swaggering susceptibility to the rocks was one that could only bode ill and that I had narrowly escaped. His susceptibility and the imminent catastrophe to which it was yoked heralded, for me, like a sediment falling to the bottom of an already muddy solution, the possibility of an identity, on the rebound, as it were, beyond thralldom to rocks and goats and her and the little ones and hovels and gainful employment of a benefit-package-laden non-freelance nature. In a sense—and in more than a sense—having staked out a claim to what I had somehow never managed to appropriate—he having gotten *there* first—his voracious and ultimately vacuous priority was leaving me no choice but to leave myself free for other, imminently more pressing concerns. He had—and on a monumental level the world will not soon forget—concretized something—love for the rocks, for their lubricious little fissures fringed with and flayed by hair—I need no longer bother to strive toward. For it—this concretized striving—was already fixed in being as rudimentary plant life was fixed in the rock-face crevices not already overrun with crabgrass: it already existed, this concretion, this something, this love, this relation, therefore there was no need to strive toward it. I resented and envied his having gotten there first at the same time as I disdained and slew him for having gotten first—and as it turned out, exclusively—to what was, after all, only one among myriad ways of being—bounded, straitjacketed, sealed off—in the world. So without knowing it what I had been seeking from the rocks was infinitely more than the rocks themselves, as creatures of finitude, could give, more than just another way of being, with them, in the bounded world.

Now as I made my way among them I was no longer seeking a relation nor caring whether what I was doing was either constitutive of or marginal to any such relation. I was completely given up to my movements as to an oration replete unto itself and to which these rocks, in all shapes, sizes, and collocations were of course warmly invited to listen even if my utmost concern must continue to be unswerving fidelity to the material, to the spirit of the material. And though the way

I moved my thigh, my arm, my groin, in relation to the movement of the rocks and their fissures and the swaying hairs deep within those fissures might seem utterly new and alien and, worse, unfounded on present experience, nevertheless in so moving—and, when the situation demanded, abstaining from movement—I felt that I was remaining irreproachably tried and true to a fatefully specific text not only antedating the moment but hoary with the antiquity of my life and the lives of all other rocks stretching to the crack of doom.

In the midst of this oratorical wandering, which, in some way, I had to admit, could be considered a transumption of his sermonizing on the run, I had least expected to lay eyes on the eldest little one, carefully and touchingly smoothing down his hair, as if after a haircut. Had he come all this way to seek me out, disregarding the remonstrances of his mom? Smiling feebly, he admitted that he had to urinate. I supervised, to make sure he did not urinate as much over himself, his new suit of clothes, as over the rocks over which, as a result of my orations, I felt I now exercised a certain proprietary right. As he urinated, meditatively he called me a name I dare not repeat, not from modesty nor fear of the censors, but simply because its obscene virulence does not remain constant over transport—does not carry over from that time and place to this, a place out of time and space. Or maybe the name hails from some other period of my life or somebody else's life or from some sequence of drunken pratfalls that can never be taken strictly speaking to constitute a life, in which case the only conclusion available to me is that there is no goat story, everybody go home, only thoughts from elsewhere commemorating slabs of incident elsewhere, modest chunks from the great floe of stories that might have been if only there had been witnesses to jeer and jeering expropriate their core of thinkable momentum. This goat song, then, if no one is prepared to go home, is a mere cento of thoughts bitten off there and chewed here. Yet only a certain kind of thought commemorating the spluttering momentum of a chip off the old block of story failed elsewhere—only a certain kind of name, unlike the name he devised for me as he urinated meditatively—has a core—nisus—that ably resists and adroitly survives rotation—translation—transplantation—to a new coordinate system of potential events. Yet what was there within these cores—these nisuses—to which I rabidly responded as consistent, consonant, consilient with their enhanced—their only real—existence elsewhere and to come, in what did not yet even begin to exist, or barely, that is, the story of the goat or of me or of me and the goat or of me and the rocks or of the rocks in the goat or of the goats in the rocks or of me within both rocks and goats. He called me an ugly name, I say, not because he truly believed I was what he called me but because the tentative exhilaration of hearing himself repeat what no doubt he had heard others call him or each other was well-nigh irresistible. And the exhilaration was in direct proportion to the hesitation, the tentativeness, the meditative tenderness with which he almost caressed the few syllables. In the very using of the name, still unmentionable, he was struggling to establish a connection between me and the name. Maybe I was the first available bystander upon which he could obtrude this name, forever fermenting within. He was striving, as the tawny arc subsided, to be semantically—angelically—correct, like a precocious *danseur noble*. If the name was applicable to me it could also be applied to him though not with equal relevance, that is, with equal force, so that the firing of the name in my direction had to be a way of expressing his rage that the name—however depreciating—could never be made to apply with equal force to him, compound, alloy, after all, of me and her. And at the same time the rage was a kind of taunting, that he had managed to escape the global relevance of such a naming, was somehow on its margin. I felt sorry for the little one, very much alone with his triumph. I turned away: the sea was truly magnificent at that hour. He mentioned, after zipping up his fly, that she had indicated, presumably in passing, her casual though forthright intention never to lay eyes on my likes again if she could help it, that she had had more than her fill, which was more oh much much more than a bellyful, of my tergiversations. I tried to smile, put my arm around him, kiss him, as much for my sake as his own. Balking he moved away, soon neither he nor any of the other little ones abounding would want to have anything to do with me. I resorted to my only remaining recourse: the rocks. Would they stand up for me as their own? One rose up slightly, to my left.

From in front it seemed, this rock face, to be pecking and bobbing forward darting as if in search of errant grains. Yet from the back it was completely retracted into itself, its last intention being to amass stray remnants. Before I could expect it to come to my assistance, that is, paint me in colors more plausible if not more ingratiating than those all heaped together on the little one's palette, it became clear I would have to conflate front and back views into a single reconciled perspective. If I had been alone, that is, not a father of little ones, I would have been perfectly willing and happy to defer to the divergence of these views, to grant that in the case of a single rock face it is not the least irregular for the front to be forever bobbing and glittering, predatory and rasorial, and the back retracted, immobile, dereistic. Such acceptance would have signalled evolutionary progress amid the whips and scorns of time. After all, if I could not accept ambiguity, lack of cohesion, how expect my little ones to thrive in such a climate? No excuse that I myself was the biggest bundle of loose ends. However my story—the goat's story—the goat's view of my story—the rocks' view of my story as the story of the goat's relation to my story—at this point demanded that I perpetrate some self-affirming violence against the landscape. At this point, after the fall of so many events in which I had played but a bit part, I should be able—so went the story line—when confronted—almost as a personal affront—with the overwhelming disjunction between a front and a back—to effect the conflation of that front and that back into an impeccable unity. As I had not been able to do, for example, when my desire for a towering crest had been baffled and blunted by the stodginess of its lower reaches.

The rock face in question sank back almost out of sight. The little one had disappeared. I thought of raging against this rock face—against all rock faces. But less than ever was I in a position to rage, having forfeited the services of the goat. So it was precisely—here was meaning, here was meaning, come at last, a benediction to all raindancing scholiasts—it was precisely at the moment of biggest temptation to let go and hold forth, to cannonade my venom to the four corners of hell for all that had and had not been done to and for me, that it was in my best interest to hold my tongue. The rock face, though subsided, was still sejant, at least with respect to its slumbering fellows, part of its allegiance to its front and part to its back with never the twain meeting if it could help it but what precisely was *it*? Another rock, an aspiring protégé, turned away from it in disgust, as on spindly legs of molten lava, that is, at first I thought it was turning away and not just from its fellow but from sea and sky and goats and all the little ones— turned away in disagreement exacerbated by a suffocating tedium. But in actual fact it was only carrying to its logical conclusion the impatience in what I suddenly realized was the first—the mother lode's— admonition. This second rock, this protégé and apostle that beings like me can only dream about inciting to a riot of eternal fidelity thereby wasting a whole lifetime in the process, was tired not of but on behalf of the first's tireless efforts to impress on all comers the futility of striving to conflate discrepant views into a unified whole. Contemplating this exemplary symbiosis I calmed down immediately and even felt sorry for having exploded at my little one, urinating, or was it he who had exploded at me. Meaning deduced, imposed, who cares, always has a calming effect.

Below, far below, little eddies of foam broke against the severally textured rock faces and collapsed into nice uniform striping riblets. The noise they made was deafening, however. I wanted to complain. I wanted to tell this rock face and its apostle, apparently bellwethers of the flock, that noise of this kind was simply impossible . . . because of my little ones or . . . because I needed to concentrate on possibilities of full-time non-freelance work. And at the same time I began to loathe myself for stooping to enumeration of specific instances—transient instances—as if the little ones would not be around for quite some time or as if there was any likelihood of my search for full-time work ever coming to an end—simply because I was convinced that presenting my case absolutely, unhinged from the circumstantial and contingent, I would, in turn, be sure to receive a pledge, commensurately absolute, that all noises would stop together, once and for all time and without this pledge being in any way contingent on the accidents of my being, that is to say, on the contingencies of my contingency. I wanted to induce—from rocks and foam—from sun and sea—an absolute fealty of capitulation to—an absolute respect for—my newfound necessary love of silence and all this without having to resort to the ostensible penury of what, in actual fact, were probably the most effective devices for pleading my case. I was afraid—I needed no goat to apprise me of as much—such contingencies—little ones sleeping, search for work—would be subsequently and inevitably surveyed so as to confirm that whatever concessions had been wrested were always in the service of said contingencies extant and more than merely latent. And the revelation of said contingencies—for it was as if I had already revealed them: speculation on the motives for my reluctance to reveal stank more of revelation than revelation itself—made me feel they—the rock and his/her apostle—must now know everything they needed to know about me and easily extrapolating to the rest inevitably decree the need for noiselessness no longer indicated. But these were not the most interesting explanations for the belief that a leaning on contingency could only damage, if not betray, my cause. I was now threatened—having revealed such contingencies—in relation not so much to these powers that appeared to be—rocks and foam and sea—as to the contingencies themselves.

They were suddenly real—the little ones, the search for work—in a way they had never been before. Recruiting them to the cause of my own well-being I, in turn, was suddenly owing them something, perhaps nothing more daunting though *under the circumstances* unassimilably overwhelming than my conviction of their abiding reality. And so that was why

And so NO

And so that was why the little one had ended up calling me a name I still cannot repeat. NO.

NO NO NO I will not give way to such meanings, to such meanings give way.

Now that I had revealed all I was miraculously no longer in need of their dispensations of noiselessness. I varied my route back, where to, I don't know, and even laughed heartily at myself varying my route for there had been no initial route on which meaningful variations could now be performed. Yet somehow my present route, which by no stretch of the imagination could be considered a variation—a deviation—had to be undergone—if it was to be undergone at all—as a variation or byproduct of the unaccountable shift in light falling, on the rocks and on everything beyond the rocks. The light was, all of a sudden, falling differently. The unanticipated fall of this light was sheathing the life of an average man—woman—child—goat—rock face—as the rise and fall of the route inexplicably and unintelligibly was evoking his—her—its average route. The light immobilized this average life or liberated it from my depths, at any rate it came gushing forth as from a fissure in the armor of habit, a fissure in fact very similar to NO

Going this average route enmeshed in an average life I was already looking back not on its actual light, the light I could touch as proof of my sanity, but the light leaking out of the fissure separating this variation in my usual route from the usual route—a light that was not of any specific time or place though evocative of a specific time and place, out of time and place. A variation in the route that at the same time was in no way different from the usual was casting my being in a mold of light very different from the usual. This was a light almost painfully abstracted from the ragged baggy substances it was obliged to clothe, a medium clogged onto itself yet distinctly rarefied and capable of wielding an infinite power of suggestion of other, better, climes. And it chose to evoke the clime most mysterious of all: life of everyday man and woman, man and woman as we, she and I, we, she and I, we, might have been now that the opportunity was blessedly and irrevocably past, which irrevocability was of course paving the way for an evocation more real than what might have been—painfully, ponderously—real for the real is always bombarded by the obfuscating contingencies particular to its version of the real. This variation in my rout[ine], by no means a variation since I had no route to vary, was—once again—that fissure, rhegma, rent, raphe, whence a new light saw fit to supplant the light prevailing and suffuse the present as future big with the mysterious life of everyday man and everyday woman—a light porous to duration yet somehow immune to the wounds of duration, brutal brute duration. This light bursting from the fissure was the light of the rock faces and the goat's flank as I had evoked them fettered and far from their call and the call of those fortunate enough to be living their life. The light liberated from the fissure was the light that incarnated the privileged beings of everyday lucky enough not to feel the need to curse the everyday. These beings—unlike me—stored the light, eternal even as it faded over the foamlets dashing against the rocks now striped with nice vertical ribs.

When I passed him, tall and stately as a goat should be, he was stroking a cleft between two rocks with his hindpaw, the hairier one. Watching fascinated I wanted to be able to reach the point of disinterestedly and unselfishly wishing them an enjoyment of such doings for if the rocks were not yet undergoing the ecstasy his tremulous and expert persistence clearly vouchsafed then it could only be my dour proximity that was responsible. He kept getting in the way—maybe it was just the furry intervention of his back and rump—of my disinterested enjoyment of their wooing. He himself cast a dour shadow. I made a concerted effort, however, to go on enjoying what I had not yet begun to enjoy, despite the sense of going on under an interdict, of being powerless to go on until he rescinded his long shadow. And yet there was also an excitement to being free of him at last, completely severed from his interest, lackluster as it was even at the best, or worst, of times. But as I felt myself moving closer and closer to the scene—of the goat inside the rocks or the rocks inside the goat—it was unclear whether I was solely responsible for propelling myself what seemed to be forward or simply yielding to whatever modicum of momentum was on loan to the world and from the world to me as a reward for mere persistence in being . . . ourselves. What was initiating this sudden movement forward, if movement forward it was and even if it wasn't—who was the initiator, world—dispensation beyond world—or I.

A sudden sensitivity to light?

This sudden sensitivity to light

About this sudden sensitivity to light

This sudden sensitivity to the light that bubbled up from a rent—raphe—seam—fissure—warp—in my program that was no rent—raphe—seam—fissure—warp at all precisely because there was no program to rend, no route to vary, no routine to exhume from the dead, this sudden sensitivity to the light—the median light of others—a mammiferous mold in which duration was as if held in reserve, at bay, paralyzed and obliged without appeal to bend to the strictures of a deathlessness suddenly intrinsic to everyday acts perpetrated by everyday folk in an everyday manner, that is to say, without extraneous aspiration—this sudden sensitivity to a stump of light, I found, and to my horror, that it was being undergone, that I was undergoing it—even if it—the stump of light—was indubitably *somewhere out there*—focused on things out there yet forever in flight from the seismic promptings of their strata—I was undergoing it as a form of incontinence, urinary or fecal, I was not sure, uncertainty being at this point my sole consolation—as at any rate a species of overflow annihilating all prior good intentions of clarity and neatness, universal husbandry and impeccable fatherhood—an overflow—an incontinence—that swelled and stained and made mincemeat of the winding sheet of abstinence in which up to now I had styled myself safely housed. I cursed him, Goat the Magisterial: absurdly I held him responsible for what was in many ways my salvation, proof of election, for how many, either on the way to work or on the way back, manage to undergo such a dissolution of all connection with the here and now in favor of the there and thence revealed as a mere stronger embodiment of the here and now. And how many among those many would have gone on to dare to reduce the rapture of such an epiphany—of such an election—we're talking here about a sudden sensitivity to a shift in the light out there undergone as an octagenarian's lowly incontinence –to a mere irritant, mere obstruction on the way to symptomless calm, symptomless order?

The rocks were facing west or in whatever direction they perceived the odor from that mold of light into which eternal everyday forms were baking to be coming. Their faces were anointed which anointedness, it seemed to me, was indistinguishable from that mode of listening peculiar to insentient things, for I remembered this from the days when she and I and the little ones strove recklessly to constitute what is known as a family, or more sickeningly, *the family*, and unaccountably she had felt comfortable enough to speak to me of these things, insentient things, even if the things she spoke of were differently insentient, and of how their listening and waiting and dreaming was a simple matter of a particular inflection of sunlight colliding head-on with an even more particular accretion of their destiny though unbeknownst to her and luckily for them said so-called destiny was nothing less than fiercest antitypy to anything of the kind. I thought I could hear voices, though hers was not mixed in the choir.

It was simply that the bulbous cumuli, having mounted in my absence, that is, absence of steady attention, and in a way Leibniz surely

would have loved, were now motioning toward me across a script
eminently worthy of a cad's decipherment just as NO

just as NO

Just as my motions to and from the rock faces had long ago
been worthy of a goat's decipherment.

And to which he, the goat, had, after a certain point, refused to
pay heed. Though had he at any time given the unmistakable sign of
wishing to pay heed. Looking to the clouds, I called to him. I don't want
to belabor, I began, as if the clouds were a specific point of contention
between us otherwise the best of buddies. And he turned away, taking
the cue, no doubt, from my utterly superfluous and self-wrecking *I
don't want to belabor*, and I, taking the cue from his turning away
dutifully and instantaneously began the business of loathing myself
even if when it is a matter of self-loathing one cannot assign to its
inception a specific point in time. By saying, I don't wish to belabor,
alluding of course to the clouds though who can say what he thought I
was alluding to, for I hadn't managed to enunciate, I don't wish to
belabor the clouds, I had merely and momentously wished to underline—for his subaudition—my superiority to the situation at hand to
whose dimensions, knowing him, he would certainly have tried to
reduce me, though who's to say what constitutes the—a—situation at
hand for frequently the situation very much at hand is very much a
camouflage, a makeshift, a handmaiden of and basely colluding with
the actual situation at hand. By saying whatever it was I said I had
hoped to elude not only the situation at hand but any situation at hand,
actual or stimulated, excrescent or inherent—any subject, object, vel-
leity, itch, hemorrhoidal or otherwise, capable of resolving itself—at his
uncannily insidious insistence—into a mad script comprising my birth
certificate, diagnosis, and death sentence beatifically conflated as I had
never been able to conflate front and back or back and front of some
old rock face rotting in the breeze. But he had quickly enough become
disgusted with my misguided loquacity—five words too many—or
maybe it was simply with the sound of my voice or my habitus as I made
ready to hold forth and so I was left, once again, to loathe myself, left to
myself as to the residuum, residualization—of myself—here and now
and forever crushed and absurdly saddled with the memory of having

attempted and failed to purvey gestures at last representative of an unassailable selfhood.

In spite of him—of being forever thrust back on the interim of a ubiquitous self-loathing—I tried to inventory what was still worthy of my rapture. But what got in the way of inventory, to say nothing of rapture, was the countervailing, overriding, and compulsive rehearsal of all the disasters that had led me here, to just this point in and out of time and space where—like the celebrated angels dancing on the head of a pin—I was expected to start learning how to make do with the unstinting computation of all I had not and never would have. In short, what got in the way of inventory was a conception of inventory as the most notorious of stigmas. Involuntarily rehearsing the succession of events culminating in this dancing head of a pin that was my life I could only curse their leaden predictability, their gorgeous uniformity, the insouciant zeal with which even now they went about sketching the hyperbolic curve of my inadequacy: Each event, each moment of each event, nothing less than a weasel paean to the rut in which I had no other option than to stink aloud.

Suddenly, here, at what I flattered myself was my very lowest point, he, the goat, turned to me and smiled, not quite a Gioconda smile but a smile, as if for the benefit of the rocks, all the rocks to which he had made love with his hooves, withers, latent udders, and not only all rocks here and now but all rocks living and dead, all rocks with faces that could at some point lay claim to having been suffused with its rays from suns occluded. He was waiting for me to make my move. It was unclear whether he was expecting me to put my foot in it or like one of those unmentionable factory bosses simply taking a pleasure almost fiendishly platitudinous in deferring once in a lifetime or blue moon to the minute, manacled, and utterly fantasmatic expertise of some under-ling—who by any other name be it wight, whiffler, quidnunc, scrub, marplot, hilding, navvy, tabellion, fellah, flunkey, or pilgarlic, wouldn't smell half as bittersweetish—some underling hitherto conveniently stashed away in a windowless corner cellule where, undeflected and almost but not quite unsurveyed, he has been able to master any number of boondoggling algorithms—in order TO enhance an already established superior status now ingredient with honest-to-goodness magnanimity while procuring himself the momentary and unequaled thrill of simpering abasement before the mouth of babes OR TO indulge in the purest and most iridescently crystalline form of base and arrant mockery known to man but never beast OR TO foment a kind of miniature saturnalia where the servants are permitted to rock their exiguous dignity to sleep in the dirty underwear of their masters. At any rate, he was waiting. Surfeited at last, he was ready and willing at last to entertain himself with my babble, whether of word or gesture. Or did he look to my utterance as the only logical culmination and turning point of his ramble among the—his—my rocks. Still speechless and in spite of myself I underwent this perceived, in other words, craved, deference as the long awaited and definitive point of demarcation between the life before and the life to come, and immediately I began to wonder how I could have perdured for so long in the ulcerating absence of such a . . . sign. Even now I felt a craving to take refuge among the rocks, or, more specifically, among their hair-clogged fissures breathing easy, breathing free, under the windy setting sun.

I continued to say nothing: I was clearly on trial and so my hardwon and now habitual vigilance, that is to say, skepticism, in the face of anything that claimed to forecast, much less embody, an "occasion" instinctively slashed the slightest upsurge of vitality, which for him—especially now, in what I took to be his decline—must stink, almost tautologically, of defiance. Yet even if I did not speak it felt as if he was all the time jeering at the incoherence of my desire, bearing down on it simply by flaunting his usual tightlippedness, which had long been able to pass in these parts for the most dazzling breviloquence. Yet at the heart of the jeering—the tightlippedness—the breviloquence—was the old and familiar urging that I leave off struggling to determine the real meaning of that jeering tightlippedness by taking a weighted average of its acceptations among the hearty rock folk and get on with the weightier business of producing analyzable specimens of craving—of desire. He was waiting to hear from me. We both knew he had to go on hearing. And if he was to go on hearing then I had to go on producing further instances of the unspeakable craving that had always managed to call into question differently and unpredictably his safety in my presence. Here he was waiting for me [having learned the hard way that only I and not the rocks could procure and prolong his professional accreditation?]—waiting to hear from me—and yet as I let the silence go on doing the dirty work of seeming to produce viable specimens of this unspeakable craving—desire—hunger—appetite imperiling for both him and me, I could not help feeling that I was advancing on though not quite fusing with a too familiar scene and that the specimens of which the scene threatened to be constituted had nothing to do with the unspeakable though they might very well be forced into having every-thing to do with it, the unspeakable. And as the silence—my silence—now our silence—went on doing its dirty work of proliferating instances of that special brand of panting prostration whose unabated virulence was sole justification for my relation to him and his to me again I could not help feeling that every instance—every specimen instance—had absolutely nothing to do with what it professed to have to do—had in fact been wrenched out of a completely alien context and without apology transplanted into this. Yet the essence—the quiddity—of the specimen instance and instant specimen had in every case and without exception first come to life—been first revealed—laid bare at last—only across and thanks to the wrenching. Of this I was sure. Sure enough to formulate the following definition: The essence was what only coming to life thereby remained constant across the wrenching. But what con-stituted this most important part of every specimen instance/instant specimen that came to incandescent life across the wrenching. He stood there and I stood there, waiting for his expression to change to one of compassion. Yet I dreaded the moment when I would recognize the all too familiar surroundings sure to be evoked by such an expression. Yet I had equally to recognize that this dread was conceivable only within the context of surroundings already almost familiar. Sure enough, seeing me stranded he was making a little gesture of welcome, already adminis-tering who knows what remedy for who knows what ills. I felt sad. For so long—too long—I had been incubating my tirade against his dour-ness in the face of my cravings, for all practical purposes quenched except insofar as they had been transmogrified into his own. During my absence, which he had managed as through an act of will, and in the course of his sojourn among rocky circumambient wastes, hadn't he supplanted me? Yet now—not so much because he was welcoming me—

who could say how much that welcome was worth?—but because one of us had managed to set in motion the first stages of my journey back—I no longer felt the urgency of the tirade. Its gravamen was shrinking in direct proportion to distance traversed. Though I was standing still. Rather, it was as if the gravamen of the tirade had always been fear— and excruciated rage at the fear—that the time and place assigned to the tirade would never come. And no doubt this enraged prostration before the unfathomableness, the vengeful unpredictability, of duration was but another aspect of the same boundless clinical picture in which such monsters as total incapacitation for work and for play in the face of his whimsical dourness also had their magical moment of violent coloration and overaggressive foreshortening.

Barely resigned to remaining the boundless clinical picture that was I, I moved toward him hoping he would unfold me in a long embrace. The way he scraped the ground with his jaw, or was it with his tail, emphasized his awareness of having been of assistance in some spheres of my problematic existence as well as the recognition of abso- lute uselessness in others. He understood—his wriggling nostril told me as much or was it his pastern—how to sustain the relation at all cost and belie his deficiencies I had striven to exaggerate my own and steer clear of all tellable feats likely to provoke the smoldering exasperation of envy. He understood, he cried out, this by butting his forehead against a not particularly attractive nearby rock face—a degenerate case of rock face, as it were. For I was now at the end of his road, far from him, his bad smell, his trembling hoofs. He turned toward the rock faces—the true rock faces, already awaiting him, I could see, at a pitch of luminos- ity to which the prospect of my own visitations can hardly be said ever to have driven them.

I stepped aside though not in his way—though not in anybody's way. Merely to help clear a path toward their wide wide embrace. He had moved off, obscured, it was over, never would I learn what consti- tuted my relation to the rocks for they were singlemindedly his. Never could I hope to deduce the nature of *his* relation from what he left behind among the undulations of their bulk. Knowing him, he was sure to leave nothing behind. Axiom: In any authentic relation nothing *is* left behind. At any rate I envied him what I easily foresaw as the ease, the listlessness even, with which he would manage to make his preferences known, for somebody like him has never any unwieldy exertions to apprehend in their or his own behalf. Cordial reciprocity must flower of itself from the inherently vibrant health of the connection. Goodbye, I muttered, noting her and the little ones too in the distance. But they were not waiting, they too were receding.

Time is the turf on which you graze.

—Capra, *Letters to the Volga Goatmen.*

Goat Song 3

Again she began to berate this tortured loathing of my life at the very
point in its—loathing's—cycle when I could feel at once that she was
grossly exaggerating and at the same time from now on it was going to
be so easy to abstain from what she had, alas, brought forth for
depiction without the least exaggeration. My paroxysm in front of the
little ones having organically played itself out—independent of whatever solatiums may have been contrived—by her—by them—to soothe
the savage breast along the way—once again, once again, I gave way to
hope. Yet here she was reminding me of all I had said and done.

When I hurled her onto the bed, onto the counterpane, onto
her beloved eiderdown, to be exact, there had been—in throwing out
the challenge of a uniqueness that had known a uniqueness of which
there was no specimen greater on this godless earth—a feeling of
incautious prodigality, located somewhere in the space between us,
between my fist, say, and the selvage of the eiderdown, of having done
wrong in not saving this truest depiction of myself for some direr and
more baldly critical occasion. And concurrent with this feeling was an
overwhelming sense of waste, at having squandered my truest depiction,
and of fear for the consequences of that squandering, of myself in my
rawest essence—and of utterest estrangement from that self insofar as it
had sanctioned the mouthing of all this perfunctory puffery about a
uniqueness that had, after all, nothing to do with my true uniqueness.

I waited: It was unclear whether the fear was of repercussion—
the slimy groggy demurral of an envious world exploding—or of un-
masking—the raging mockery of one intolerant of all gratuitous aggrandizement. Not that the story necessarily begins here. This beginning, like
all beginnings, is a mere placeholder against the real beginning or its
impossibility. She told me to go out and find work, any work at all. I
knew where I was intending to go. My hand on the doorknob, she cried,
loud enough for the children to hear, that she had managed nevertheless
to overcome or at least mute her hatred of the moments before. She had
hated me, she acknowledged, in response to particular movements,
gestures, stalemates, not these but those. I perceived her peculiar exultation—for it is undeniable that grandeur accrues to even the lowliest soul
enmeshed in the making of fine distinctions—at apprising me of this her
new differentness from—transcendence of—some ostensibly prior self

that had probably hated for far longer than she bothered or wished to admit and was still going strong. In short, we were both more than grazed by the pathos inherent in her involuntary discovery that she was a contourless infinite rage no longer, at least as far as I was concerned— even if—especially since initially she had wanted nothing so much than for that rage to be all of her, all there was to her, forever. We both felt the pathos of looking at her at last from without—from a vantage—but whose—a coign—but whose—reducing, rather distilling, her to the modest dimensions of a specific resignation willing to go forward even if it had to be by my side. At a given juncture [no localizing it] there was no more exaltation answerable to no one, nothing further to be squeezed— to be had—from the boundless rage I provoked. The only exultation still to be had was that pursuant to the making of fine distinctions—between rage and rage transcended, looked back on, for example—and between the self that had raged and the self looking back on the self that had raged. The little ones were yelping: They did not understand how potent fine distinctions could be. For them there had once been rage and so there must be rage forever. And who among us had the resources to prove them wrong or even subject to redirection.

And not only were the little ones yelping but the very rafters wobbled as if they had caught a chill. Which little scene, that, presumably, of departure only further convinced me of what I already knew, namely, that no one element, in my life at least, had any significance— all were without exception trivial to bursting—but only the warring solicitation for my attention of each and every incompatible exalting or plunging me deeper than the nethermost pit of hell to the degree that its own self-appointed urgency of the moment managed to confer a certain status conspicuous to my badgered eyes. I was the besieged breadwinner who could not live by bread alone. So I encouraged her scolding, the heartrending cries of my offspring, and the insinuating wince of the panes and the rafters—incarnating the scalding commentary of previous generations and those to come—as I encouraged the rocks toward which at this very moment I had every intention of making my way, job or no job, though they stood absolutely in no need of such encouragement—I needed them all in the name of some cento of butt-ends, surely the closest I would ever come to a story.

Stepping into the dour dewy twilight I felt proud of myself for not having lashed back at her for having just now lashed out or back at me, for what was all this talk about a job, any job, but a lashing back, even if such praiseworthy abstention was not to be admired as anything more than an involuntary admission of fatigue or proof that at this point in time I was too much in need of compassion, at least its signs and signals, and seeking it far more avidly than I secretly believed was compatible with my uniqueness, to be capable of doing my utmost to reduce whatever remained of her autonomous will to a cinder of my own. I was off and running, though walking, toward the rocks, my beloved rock faces invariably deployed to set off their hair-clogged fissures and grainily undulating surfaces to best advantage. But before permitting myself to set eyes on the rocks I tried to regain a hold on myself so as to have a plausible self to bring to the rocks. As I looked out past them toward the sea, also undulating but not in such a way as to provoke onlookerly frenzy, some of the little ones passed by. Feeling them behind me, though, strictly speaking, they were directly in front of me—her envoys, her scullions, her streetcorner nuncios, their clamor challenging every step of a progress toward reassumption—could I use that word?—of the only identity that counted for something—one acceptable or at least intelligible, whether commending or revulsed, no matter, to the rocks—feeling them behind me I not only went on staring but told myself point blank that I had every right to be doing so, fusing with the offing, as it were—so purplish, so clogged with reflected rack— even if telling myself as much interfered strenuously with the actual staring and fusing. As they trooped back I went on telling myself, but alas no longer point blank, that I was every inch a sea looker—a sea looker, rather than an amorphous clod at the mercy of whoever and whatever cared ungraciously to catch him with his seaward-looking pants down and out—and as a sea looker, salty and seasoned, I should as a matter of course of course be expected every now and then to entitle myself to immersion in certain subsidiary pleasures of which sea looking *per se* naturally was to be numbered first among the most—as among the least—prominent.

What these onlookers—these gory onlookers—to whom I was, by the way, totally indifferent [the little ones were gone, had been replaced by fresh dispatches]—needed to know and yet must never know was that sea looking was vital to a project whose details I was not yet at liberty for public edification to misrepresent. Suffice it to swagger and sneer that when at last I was in a position, or better yet, a posture, to reveal all—well—the very foundations of sand and sea would as a matter of course be rocked to *their* very foundations. There was no one to assist in the reconstitution of my identity, no one to say, for example, Of course, in response to my, Excuse me, as I edged my way politely past them toward the rocks as I would have done on, say, a crowded subway platform since, unfortunately, there was no one whose stance could be construed as in the slightest way barring my passage. I turned and watched the little ones disappear—superseded by other—the truly gory—onlookers—far beyond the rocks, in the direction of a steep ravine sparsely blotched with sprucelike vesture.

I became aware of my expression, dreaded beginning to resemble all those I had been trained—by her, even by the little ones mimicking her—once their seemingly random flickers of wild impatient contempt could be construed as alarmingly buttressed by the coherent world view latent in the imperturbability of brow and upthrust of buttocks, to view as mad. The troop of little ones fading out of sight offended my world view: I was overwhelmed with a cold suspicion, as if such trooping off without express permission, even if there was nothing I so much desired, was aimed only at fooling me, making the very earth recede beneath my feet. And even if I knew as well as I knew anything that this trooping off—of little ones pursued by gory onlookers or of gory onlookers pursued by little ones—was a purely self-referential gurgling that had absolutely nothing in the world to do with me, still I received—underwent—it as something of which I was obliged—more than obliged, constrained—to cure them, my little ones, whom, even when I neglected them most frightfully, which was most of the time, I was nevertheless righteously—pietistically sure—I was already managing to adapt to their rightful and exalted station. Clearly, then, there could be no gurgling, self-referential or otherwise, since japing of any kind, I knew from bitter experience, boded incurably ill for later mandatory and undeviating dedication to the golden mean of hearths and profits. Yet all along I also knew I was seizing on their trooping only to invest it with a meaning or, let us say, an inflection that positively did not—could not—belong to it belonging as it must to some other specimen from somebody or something else's repertory of instances—of instant incidents—of course unassimilable to this particular situation.

Yet even if that other specimen was not assimilable to this particular situation the meaning imposed on it—made to belong to it—in other words, the thought, T, I had managed to have about it, S, long before was—had to be—assimilable—once again as thought T but a thought T now about situation S', the trooping away of gory little ones. Against my better judgment I was discovering that thought T—about situation—specimen—manifestation—incident—event—S—could with minor adjustments, whose incidental difficulties must only redound to its greater glory—be made to apply to situation—specimen—manifestation—incident—event S', reducible to the little ones trooping off in company of severally gory onlookers. I had to act—now. For who could say when the opportunity might again arise for me, a mere wight, to have this thought—to produce it like a trump card—to apply it like a poultice—to have this thought T about—that is to say, impose this thought on and against—a situation—event—incident—specimen—perturbation—to the slightest degree deemable as likely—some disturbance event S' in any degree homologous to the S that had, far away and long ago, originally provoked it. And especially since the present situation, that is, S', was well-nigh unprompted going out of its way to accommodate itself to the thought, T, how could I bear to leave the latter without a domicile, however rudimentary. But even if, as I was beginning to suspect, the present situation, S', was vastly different from—absolutely irreducible to—its predecessor, S, responsible for the initial upsurge of thought T somewhere and some time out there in the great world beyond the rocks—when it was not nor could it ever have been a question of amassing butt-ends suitable for the stuffing of some cento—even if S' was anathema to S as S to S', thereby bringing to the fore a—the supreme—slew of unanswerable questions, namely, What does thought T bring to the event E that provokes it? does T replace E for all time? does it eat away, slowly or with colossal rapidity, at it? does T subsist proudly and compatibly at E's side, the two like a pair of lamb chops on the same pewterized plate kept warm for the imminently returning master of the house?—even if S and S' intersected nowhere still the transplantation of T(S) into a new and unfamiliar context as— lo and behold!—T(S') had to be considered a plausible—a justifiable— an eminently desirable—stratagem insofar as some core of articulable anxiety redolent of T remained constant over the transplantation. And NO

in a NO sense, in more NO than one sense, NO in NO every NO NO NO sense—so I was suddenly discovering—the thought—a thought—the "T" thought—could only begin veritably to exist—in other words prove its mettle, that is to say, its essence—only over a transplantation that simultaneously stretched and compressed its essence wide of an inevitably festering home context. I was discovering that thought T, whose meaning I had already or was just about to impose on trooping situation S', was only just beginning, transplanted elsewhere—to this elsewhere—to be authentically a thought. Fortunately expelled from the initial context S, with which it must at all cost refuse any further identification—in which already it had been far too long festering and would doubtless have been doomed to fester evermore, in other words, go on masking the essence of its vital core amid a pullulating cluster of lame because too appropriate contingencies, if what I dare to refer to as my story had not come along—the thought— my thought—thought T— was turning into itself at last. I or my story had managed to uproot and tear it free of what erroneously had been presumed to be vital to, indistinguishable from, its being—had been presumed to *be* its being—and was only just now beginning to show its true colors of irrelevance. Not me but my story, then, had managed to uproot and effect its extradition, for what was I but my story and what was my story but the dizzying agglomeration of just such butt-ends recruited from everywhere and nowhere, but preferably nowhere, to fill this or that gap, none of which gaps strictly speaking qualified as gaps but for the butt-ends subsequently filling them. What was my story but a *function*, the mapping of butt-ends from their domain's untroubled chaos to some far-off range of decreed sequential continuity.

Can I help it, I cried out, almost to the disappearing little ones, still disappearing, sometimes reappearing depending on subtle shifts in the topography, can I help it if for me a story is no story and will never qualify as one unless incessantly caulked, preferably beyond recognition, that is to say, created from scratch, using butt-ends from elsewhere, the rationale, that is to say, the immediate provocation, for such caulking being less the conviction that the same thought can apply to more than one situation or disturbance event than the frenzied premonition that said thought is not quite appropriate to and will never be made to fit the new—any new—context, no matter how apparently homologous the homologs initially appeared, and so vengefully and with continuous unabated frenzy must be made to fit. It became clear, then, that my stories, all of them, had to be characterized as *wrenchings from* rather than *fittings into* place. But I had to admit, though I did not broadcast this in the direction of the disappearing brood, in behalf of the wrenching and twisting and turning with their attendant commos-laden objurgations to the effect that nothing ever fits or works at the precise moment one needs it to fit or work on this eternally clogged shithole of an earth, deceptively shiny as a hemorrhoid—in their behalf there is a ravaged joy forever at work thwarting and thereby exalting the ingenuity never quite risen to the occasion of extirpating and ousting and usurping and reinstalling and supplanting so that thought without context may fit new context. And so for the purpose of this my goat song the retreating of the troop of little ones, continuing to weave their way in and out of the elephantine crotch of gorier onlookers, appallingly neglected yet uncomplaining, had to be viewed or undergone—as once long before somebody's ranting and raving, or farting and shitting, or effeminization replete with pumps, peacock feathers, and high-pitched palmistry, had, by me or somebody like me or too little like me, to be viewed or undergone—according to the minute specifications of thought T, that is, as an unconscionable travesty and mockery aimed at nothing less than my self-respect or as a mere directionless self-indulgent babbling on the lowest level of locomotion or as neither or as both.

From the way they wended their way it did not appear likely I would be missed by the little ones, not that they had ever missed me during my regular excursions, only this time it looked as if they might very well miss me *less than ever before,* for at last I was in the domain of the story as a cento of butt-ends and as sop to the story all that happens or fails to happen in its domain happens necessarily in what may be termed—and not for lack of a better expression—the hyperlative mode. Why else would I have chosen to be leased out to that domain. Maybe the little ones had had enough of these wrenchings of their doings, pretty much reducible to their comings and goings, well beyond recognizability merely to satisfy the anxious specifications of thoughts—my thoughts—that strictly speaking had absolutely nothing to do with these doings. In addition, I was jobless, homeless, familyless, hot in pursuit of what could only spur me to vaster privations, to say nothing of the vastest privation of all: sheer indifference to consequences. To silence what I was just beginning to undergo as a ripple of inquietude on the surface of that indifference I announced: All I want is to stroke the rocks, to run my fingers first alongside then within their hairy fissures. They were no longer visible nor were there any more second-generation gory onlookers to enliven my quest. And yet despite the fact that nothing seemed to be happening either inland or upon the high seas I began suddenly to undergo a sense of urgency all out of proportion to present stimuli, to any tangible wealth of accrued meanings requiring storage or at least localization. With no situation—even—incident— disturbance—perturbation—in sight I was nonetheless overwhelmed with thoughts concerning other situations which thoughts could and with only the tiniest effort, I was sure, be transplanted into my present context, that of imminent surrender to the rocks. I was overwhelmed then out of all proportion to my status for I had none having no vocation. The rocks, how could they be my vocation? I was as I had always been with respect to the rocks: Under the interdict. Nevertheless amid this total absence of materials, to say nothing of a vocation spacious enough to store such materials, I was overwhelmed with the unwieldly superfetation of too many goads to some future course of production. I had all the symptoms of a man in the middle of a project—feelings of sliminess, reprehensibility, unwashedness—though none of the tremors of output.

In spite of myself I was anticipating success though how could success or the lack of it enter into prostration before and surrender to the rocks. But I could not help applying the criteria of a vocation to what was no more than an improvisational abasement. And how could I be thinking of success for him—for myself—after having mistreated her and neglected the little ones. So mistreatment and neglect had been perpetrated with one purpose in mind: To ensure that when entrepreneurial success became undeniable I would be unable to relish what was flagrantly and irreversibly contaminated by whatever unspeakably I had lent myself to in rage at its absence. Mistreatment and neglect had been sustained so as ultimately to be thrown into high and shattering relief against the backdrop of a success that however rawly craved could only dwindle to insignificance through the contrast. But there was no—never would there be—a question of success. Success did not mesh at any point along the serrated edge of my quest for the rocks. Or rather, the concept of success did not mesh at any point along the serrated edge of the concept of my quest. Though who was to say that success might not apply to construction of the story of the rocks once, that is, the story showed itself amenable to the interminable intercalation of butt-ends.

I tried to shrug off the overriding prospective sourness of success where I was concerned or where the rocks were concerned or where I deep inside the rocks was concerned and concentrate once again on the sea. For I was free to formulate sea and its everchanging sky in any way I chose. Free to formulate—dizzyingly free, when in actual fact a constraint of innumerable crazily intersecting pathways traversing now dread of the death of my relation to her and the little ones, now mourning for same, now gasping anticipation of self-obliterating lust for the rock faces, now shame at such a gasping, was at all times driving forward that formulation and thereby decreeing what was ultimately to constitute my bag and baggage, bed and breakfast, of formulated sand, sea, foam, breakers, naked bodies writhing simulated gratification—of, in a word, tenderfooted yearning. I was unfree to see the sea as I wished. But it was far too early—in the story—in the story—to perceive that I was very much under a cloud. Back to the hovel I turned for some strange reason or no reason at all. For some strange reason or no reason at all: this is the stuff of which the space between butt-ends is made. She advanced toward me. When I could taste her sweet breath in my mouth she said, You see, I don't want to live through you. That is why I packed you off—to do your own work and let me do mine. Something about the phrase, *live through you*—that was the phrase, wasn't it?—suggesting—decreeing—that I was the husband and she the wife, set me on fire, made me, in other words, want to triturate myself to unrecognizability rather than be subjected to—living proof of—its relevance. Incineration was the only conceivable escape from the implications of such a description unironically planting me right smack in the middle of being. For there was nowhere I less wanted to be than in being and she knew that, she had to know that, by now. This phrase, like so much of her chatter, was ponderously redolent of quasi-technical jargon, psychiatric or culinary, which I always made it a point to undergo in the ironic mode and thereby flushed clean of any residually hearty Bavarian chocolate-cherry-cheesecake-flavored positivism. For example, the phrase *existential malcontents* as applied to Gulag survivors or neonatal drug fiends filled me with delight, that is, insofar as it rebounded on the precise and exquisite imbecility of the utterer, generally overaccredited, professionally speaking. I should mention, though in extenuation of what precisely? that even before she opened her mouth, long before I could smell her burning breath or her thighs, she had already advanced upon and over me, long before I could even begin to entertain the possibility of conceiving of such a possibility. Her advance turned out to be the incarnation of my anticipation of that advance but long long before I knew I was harboring such an anticipation.

As if, I replied, you or for that matter anybody could live through me, through my achievements. At the word *achievements* I burst into uncontrollable laughter. I knew she would never stoop to immersing herself in thereby feeding the laughter though I also knew she certainly shared the sentiment that had prompted it. She waited, each standing his ground over a vastly different ground. So tense and uncomfortable did this make me, her having actually come to me with what for her was an invincible and ironclad determination never to want to live her life through mine, that I could pay only the most cursory attention to the beautiful story element accruing from it and having something vaguely yet vibrantly in common with standing over the steaming parapets after battle only to find oneself mincingly importuned by the demands of the domestic hearth, etc., etc., etc.

I was too obsessed with getting away from her—from her phrase—to properly live this beautiful butt-end and story element. So that I had to be grateful for the tense uncomfortableness that made me obsessed with getting away. In tearing me away from my beautiful butt-end the tense uncomfortableness of my obsession managed to preserve it from the indelible taint axiomatically consequent to living it, living through it. And so I was able to go on for as long as I wished catching heartrending glimpses of that butt-end's obstructed-promised-land inaccessibility. My tense uncomfortable obsession with getting away from her and back to the rocks—though it was difficult to pinpoint the former as cause of the latter, as in any way connected with the latter—had, I decided, furnished me with something far better than a story element to live and thereby grind down to the nothingness of feeble commemoration. Heaping shards of gnarled regret it gave me, more appropriate when all was said and done to one anticipating—seeking—annihilation at the hands of those faces. How much longer could I have gone on maintaining the fiction that I was just about to embody one and as eternally stable as its evolution across the frontiers of my unlocalizable context? Absurd. More and more absurd the closer I came to annihilating prostration before the rock faces I wanted mightily to crave.

She saw me shaking, eager to move on. But she was incapable of saying, I see the symptom—craving for the rocks—is making you tremble. Don't alter your way of life to suit the vagaries and velleities of that symptom. Don't abandon me simply because the symptom seems to be telling you to move on well past the groans and giggles of the little ones. Stand your ground, stick to your big guns. I began to hate her for not saying any of this and saving me thereby from myself until I realized that these craved constructions were not being meanly and purposefully withheld: They were simply inconceivable to her powers of telling. Nor could she have said, were the sun setting before her very eyes, No telling what the final recrement will look like: I see from your harried gaze that you, meaning me, expect the final chaos to have a cumulative—a well-nigh lustral—impact—to be an agglomerative summarizing of the day's racky flaw-driven phantasmagoria. Do not expect: There is every possibility the final burst will be affirmatively and excessively nonrepresentative of the succession of disarrays that preceded it. So stop expecting a scripted summarizing counsel from the clouds as to how to conduct the rest of your life. Stop expecting, I concluded, whispering to myself, so inconceivable a telling from her likes.

I needed her to be telling me things of this sort, about the machinations of my symptom and about the sunset and what and what not to be expecting from it. But she was not withholding: things like these were, to her, simply inconceivable. So I had no choice but to move on, perhaps the rocks would be capable of saying what I needed somebody to say, or some animal given to roaming their faces at all hours of the night and day. Certain things simply had to be said if I was to go on but to be said they had after all to be sayable and sayable they were evidently only for specific beings or for specific things blessedly not quite acceded to the status of beings. Whatever I needed her to be saying—that if, for example, I was intending to give myself to the rocks—although she insisted it was the goats I was after—then my giving should not conform to the contour of any categorical symptomal concept of a giving—could come only from one or ones not quite on the threshold of being. All such formulations were within the purview only of those striving in vain to be within the purview of any purview. And what if all these formulations dolefully craved were though ostensibly dissimilar in fact an endless repetition each of the other, a unisonal and glaring monotony giving tinny almost imperceptible voice to the old hunger to be and the dread, given the consequences—so foreseeable and yet so alarming—of so being.

I know where you're off to: the goats. You prefer their bodies to mine. And in an undertone: The bony little skulls flecked with dried excremental hairs. Here she was, failing me once more, over and over again, though not in her inadvertently implicit condemnation of a symptom—a craving—a hunger—a desire—I couldn't even begin to pretend to claim as my own (rocks), not even in her explicit condemnation of what for purposes of narrative thrift with its grim obeisance to institutionalized meaning must pass for its obverse (goats)—but in her recoil from the challenge of saying certain needed and eminently sayable things. *I know you prefer the goats to me* maddened because it usurped the space rightfully belonging to these eminently sayables. I wanted to get away, to the rocks, at last, though not quite sure of what must ensue from such intercourse—to bring to a boil, at any rate, whatever was in the way of being brought to a boil, so that I might have done at last with all this preparation for prostration and annihilation.

The only antidote for event, should it turn out that event was indeed to be born of a collision between—the space between—me and the rocks, the rocks and me, was its inevitability and the way of that inevitability could be eased only by me—by my forthright and thoroughly self-possessed impatience of refusal to collaborate in and prepare for the advent of event. Only event's inevitability was capable of bringing to a halt inevitably and all too typical failed construction of the edifice of manly and stalwart and steadfast and unflinching contention with it. Among the rocks—among the event of my collision with the rocks—among inevitable expiration of that event—lay my only hope of leaping out of the stagnant present whose demon she for one had been shown incapable of exorcising through the saying of certain sayables and into the future and by so leaping who would be foolhardy enough to deny that I couldn't help but accelerate its—the future's—transmogrification into that golden age sure to liberate me from the mortal coil of far more than a brute duration. Only in my desperation I was forgetting that for years, decades, centuries, millennia, brute duration had managed most successfully—almost effortlessly—to resist any such transpositions, much less transmogrifications, even—espe NO—even—espec NO—even—especially—when roweled ever so subtly and every so often by my craving for same.

Yet precisely because she had proved incapable of saying certain things—*the* certain sayable things—guaranteed to save me from myself, that is to say, from the rocks, that is to say, from myself—things—but vastly different things—were happening much faster, faster and faster, than ever they would have happened if for once she had managed to rise to the occasion. She refused to budge. She was still beside me looking off in the direction of the sea and her mere presence—its embodied dead weight of disapproving resistance—its slag of skewed imploration that I return straight away to the fold, to her and the little ones, and furnish thereby incontrovertible proof at last of a definitive repudiation of this absurd allegiance to rock faces masking one even more insidious and insidiously redolent of goats and goatish cries—her mere presence with its appalling upsurges of palpable interdiction was suddenly provoking—had suddenly provoked—un-earthed—a premonition of pleasure so vast I could barely conceal the tremblings, the burning in the bowels, to which it gave rise. The boundlessness of bliss was upon me which boundlessness was in no way jeopardized by the fact that this bliss had come to birth as not its own metempsychosis but a mere contradictious byproduct and outpouching of the monumental grimness inhearsed among her ribs and sinews. Still I felt overwhelmed, defenseless, unworthy, in the face of so much . . . fluidity devolving without any visible sign of imminent subsidence on one natively so ill-equipped even for its contemplation from afar. It is therefore understandable that in my dread, my shame, I should wish to reduce what boundless in bliss threatened to inhabit a duration commensurately boundless to a mere interim and jumping off place. This prospect of fluid bliss sprung full blown from the forehead of contradistinction to the ever-embodied prohibition of her blowsy presence—fluid bliss as the brainchild, so to speak, of prohibition—was simply too too overwhelming. What to do with this bliss, already upon me, where put it, where do you put bliss, how stave it off, how tell bliss to know its place and keep it? And so I was managing to create a rent in the fabric of this bliss, toxic, fluid, and boundless. And before I was even done creating the rent immediately it had to be repaired as soon as possible, as soon, that is, as I could see my way clear to having done with—getting over—what was now the sole obstacle in the way of thorough-going repair, namely, bliss boundless and ebullient, without rent and without flaw. The rent had the shape of fear, fear, specifically, that for all this premonitory superabundance among the rocks themselves—the only context for the conceivability of bliss, toxic or otherwise—there would be no symptomatic slobbering whatsoever—by me in front of them or by them in front of me, in short, no slobbering whatsoever, no thwarted upsurges, no—bliss event, that is to say, toxic, fluid, and boundless bliss localizable somewhere but with no event to contain it—against which to titrate—to yoke it NOR even a lofty, towering, inaccessible, and impregnable model bliss event against and in deference to whose example its own virulence might be wrested, most judiciously, drop by drop. So I had no choice but to hurry on back or hurry on down to the rocks, even if I was already very much in the heart of the rock district albeit in another—an alien—capacity in order to resolve this matter of whether or not where the rocks and I or I and the rocks were concerned there could be a bliss event as well. I knew there could be bliss since what was this pouring out of every orifice and then some if not bliss but could there be a bliss event, bliss as event, that is to say, something gradual, orderly, divisible, intercalatable, acquirable in installments of telling, that is, self-loathing. But now, partitioned among my million and one tasks, I was fit to foresee pleasure, the prospect of pleasure, more than pleasure—bliss—toxic, boundless, and fluid bliss—only as an obstruction, a wily enfeeblement, en route to preparation for active intervention in resolving this question of whether, where the rocks and I were concerned, it was meaningful, much less self-evident, to speak of event, bliss event, unfolding in installments recuperable by a telling. And with all my heart and soul I believed in this problem, or rather, my overwhelming fear of boundless toxic bliss and where it might lead me made haste to believe in this problem *wherever* it might lead me and in all the legwork its resolution surely would demand—even if elsewhere on my person I was absolutely convinced such a problem had been concocted cockeyed and slapdash merely to retrieve me from such a fear. All things considered, boundless bliss, engendered initially in almost lackadaisical contradistinction to her bulldozing embodiment of purest prohibition, was now expanding indigenously beyond anybody's wildest dreams least NO of NO all NO NO NO least of all mine. And I had no intention of riding the wave of its temerity because I could not help suspecting that after the ball was over and following the inevitable crash there would be no *where* on which to fall back and, more important, that for all this verbigeration on so timely and topical a theme something else might be—might very well have been—at stake and involuntarily transplanted to the context—wrenched into conformity with the meaning—transmogrified into the very name—of—toxic, boundless, fluid—bliss.

I did not want to plan a strategy for determining whether between me and the rocks anything vaguely like unto a relation still subsisted. Planning implied there might or might not be event in store. Might or might not: I did not have a high tolerance for ambiguity: invariably I underwent the ambiguity of things *out there* as retribution for crimes mounted within. This state of affairs—this possible absence of bliss event—could very well have been avoided if only I had managed never to succumb to the egregious luxury of coinciding with myself and managed simply to be or to become an other—that other sketched by her ubiquitous exasperation, for example. I did not want to plan a strategy, I simply wanted to find myself among the rocks as soon as possible even if I was already among the rocks. Strictly speaking, the soothing prospect of imminent bliss should have legitimated—naturalized—the appropriateness of a planning interval. Unfortunately, any soothing prospect—even of sated genitalia—only managed to throw into bolder relief the everpresent craving to throw myself out of the nearest window. There were no windows in these parts. In sum, once again she or I or life or the rocks or the goats or a fatal admixture of some or all or none was proving incontrovertibly that for someone like me, although there was no one like me, whatever innocent diversions the eternal sumpter saw fit to deliver up—in homage to my anguish—on an overdressed trencher were always far more of a weight around my already colloped and carbuncled neck than that ostensibly insupportable anguish it—the trencher—had been flown in to mitigate. The sea was absolutely still though the tide was still ebbing—on a strandscape of second-rate novelties. Looking at her I inferred—from her smiles, her playful jabs at my ribs—that she was taking my eagerness to be gone as sign that at last I wanted to turn myself into a hardworking member of society, that I wanted to test my manhood as one probates a will, and not just my manhood but my likelihood and my maidenhood too, for her sake and the little ones'. A solid citizen, the local doctor, was now visible as a brownish blob, a kind of cosmic liver spot, on or against, however you prefer, on or against the horizon, itself a mere liver spot against some background still to be defined, in other words, emancipated from chaos. I wondered if she too had seen him, she must have, for she said, At first you'll have to be careful. No recreational or remedial reading, for example. But once your colleagues begin to know and love you the way I hope to someday—once, that is, you begin to *make your name in the company*—then at that future date alas unspecifiable but no sooner those very idiosyncrasies that might—if disclosed at first—have been the forerunner of so much unwarranted misprision will be accepted, more than accepted, actively solicited, and not just at company or even public functions, as treasured manifestations of your indispensability to the team effort. At this very moment, though great is my loathing of props and especially props greasily and gaudily prompt, even if drolly subhuman and in no way assailable as contraptions of my own—at this very moment I must acknowledge that he, the local worthy, the liver spot in question, saw fit to make his appearance, replete with shako, yataghan, and monocle, and followed by what looked like wife, mother, mother-in-law, and a brood of little worthies-to-be, gorgeously attired. Her involuntarily—though who's to say for sure if indeed involuntarily—adoring look meant little less—and little more—than, What a perfect harmonizing of the infrastructures of play, love, and work is embodied in this man, almost superhumanly serene as he goes about esemplasticizing all human potential as we presently know it into one great shining forth. I looked away but felt her gaze still upon him, goading me toward self-protective disparagement of all he oh so heroically embodied in order to gain admission once again into a vicious circle of mutual recrimination that could only leave us both shattered and the little ones bereft. She wanted to draw me out toward enactment of that rancor at the heart of her essentially weasel paean to this hilding.

I pointed to the rocks, still not looking her way. She had the good doctor and his clan, I had the rocks. But why did I entertain, even subliminally, the expectation that merely pointing in their direction would automatically contaminate her with the transcending awe that puts triumphs such as his in their rightfully puny perspective. I was forced to speak, still not looking, though my voice was so loud it must seem I was pouring out my heart to him and his: For one in love with the rocks—ensign of a universal yearning—getting on with them can never mean getting on simultaneously with the blissfully proper integration of play, love, and work. Such a perfect tuning of the escapement does not in this case guarantee maximum output—for those, that is, still preoccupied in our day and age with such abasements—and if by some off chance—some gyration of the ratchet wheel—it does, then that output is necessarily offal. Don't you find, my dear—still not looking her in the eye—this harping on output dreadfully vulgar, to say nothing of all the babble about this, that, and the other stone ground up to perfection in the gizzard of good citizenry—dreadfully vulgar, that is, in a realm that deserves far better press: the rocks. Here I gestured rockwards or what I took to be rockwards with a grandiosity of corporeal unfolding requiring, elbow glued to rib cage, that my forearm move, or rather skate, through an arc of sixty degrees, palm of course maximally outstretched toward the target of my veneration. A realm—inferring her drugged venomous look—of sensuous serpent forms incessantly dying and reviving though riddled with hairy fissures, each strand as seductive as the hottest orchidaceous tongue. Maximum output in such a realm would necessarily, surely you see what I mean, engender monsters.

No response: last I saw she was trailing after. The peacock feather atop the worthy's shako nodded in the breeze. Still it was as if she was beside me, gnawing at my rib cage. But there was no remaining next to her for her presence could only prevent me from thinking that thought by which—and in a single fell swoop—I was transported beyond life—our life—and she—from my coign in that ether—metamorphosed into her inverse, that is, some eminently forgivable being whose naked surface area hatched with arrises caught the light in a manner reminiscent of rock faces at their most doeful, most exquisite.

Now I was ready to return—to the rocks and their den of iniquity. At last I was ready to return for I always made it a practice, in other words, out of the blue I was discovering how valuable it might be to make it a point to manage to make it a practice, to precede my visits to the lair of snarling tongues with some humiliating denigrating annihilating ordeal such as had been for example embodied minutes before in the interplay of her and shako and brood of worthies and sun setting over brood of worthies and yataghan and monocle and mother and mother-in-law and last but not least over her aghast sycophancy so as then to be able to fly to those snarling tongues on the wings, as it were, of a true devastation wrought by senior colleagues or their like, though in my present state who wouldn't qualify as senior colleague or its like. At last my hunger—my craving—for the rocks was a real craving because inseparable or indistinguishable from rage at the devastation wrought. My hunger—my craving—was my rage: No. I was discovering that the humiliation and torment that such devastation left in its wake—

the undefinable ague induced by some senior colleague intent on proving, unbeknownst often to himself but through some telltale Legrandi-
nian undulation of the hip or retraction of the pupil to me unmistak-
ably, I was no more than my bloody excretions or at best a rotting
prosthesis of the hip or an unemptied health-club spittoon—could be
made to serve as foothold—and in the real world, no less—for only NO
humiliation, disgust NO, torment NO, ague, constitute the real world
NO, with rocky cravings and fissured hungers little more than a prop, a
marginalium, a scrappable quiddity of placeholding lunacy, well
beyond whose meagre mangled intermittent blaze subsisted the true
source—the true sustenance—namely, the good doctor and all senior
colleagues like unto that lordly locum of a fart. All for nought, then,
this craving for the rocks, or rather, the construction of this craving,
which even minutes before I still had had every intention of striving to
undergo as what it might yet be—an overwhelming subversion of all
conceivable structures of pursuit of the Golden Mean, such a one as the
good doctor had, no doubt, spent every night of his waking life mastur-
bating over—all for nought for the craving was nought but a fixture, a
dislocation—a not even radical subluxation of the real problem, the real
symbiosis, whose well-being might be to some slight degree enhanced
by the targelike fiction of the rocks as my big dark and dirty secret. It
now would be much simpler, given my need for a placeholder, an
instrument, to stick my finger up my nose or ass when nobody was
looking and when, after all, was anybody who was anybody ever looking, at least in the way that my craving for shame demanded they look.
In short, the rocks were—had been—were a fungible interim device, a
toy detonator concocted by the junior colleagues according to the
specifications of the senior colleagues for my occasional use and particularly at those moments when these tidy thugs, senior and junior,
stepped out for a bit of harmless meditation or to slake the needs of
their surely well-nigh unlovable loved ones. The rocks were to keep me
busy until they were able to resume bothering themselves about my
abasement.

But there was another possibility: What if both the craving for
the rocks and addiction to finding myself in situations inviting invidious
comparison with those portly senior colleagues [the doctor was by no

means overweight, in fact, he was the lithe, supple, slender potential pride of any fashionable tennis club]—situations with which my high-road was already copiously bestrewn thanks to her, thanks to her, for attracting such paragons as the doctor the way a lightbulb attracts the imminent dust of elytra, was it any wonder she was able to yoke me with a prestidigitator's ease to the very situations in which they felt most at home?—What if, I say, this craving and that addiction were self-suffi-cient fulgurations of the same bedrock disease? Though if fulgurations symptomatic of the same psychic ache there was no reason why neces-sarily they had to be each self-sufficiently unawares of the other's independent upsurge, with no contact between them—with no neigh-borly potentiation each of the other's virulence—reporting, as it were, only to the most subterranean springs within the innermost circle of disease-entity headquarters. To explore these possibilities required com-plex testing on a multitude of variables, as the experts say. What if I murdered all my senior colleagues? Would I then continue to need the rocks? If no, then craving for the rocks clearly must be relegated to the status of mere byproduct and fortuitous lubricant of this need to abase myself before and behind senior colleagues on and off my highroad. But what if, senior colleagues conveniently wiped off the face of the earth, need for the rocks remained as overwhelming as ever, greater even, with only the thinnest penumbra of dread that such need, craving, hunger, desire, very well might—due to this definitive absence of a stabilizing foothold in imminent shadowy judgment, that is, some stinging—excru-ciating—humiliation still and forever fresh in my groin and urging as analgesic excrucation still more stinging—very well might end up hav-ing no beginning and no end? In that case, the senior colleagues and their entourage of toy-concocting flunkeys could with security be con-sidered a mere mangled shadow of buoying though vastly overrated anti-succor. Although it was still quite possible—quite compossible—that the two most powerful incitements to rock craving if not rock pleasure could turn out to be the ubiquity *and* the definitive absence of the senior colleagues, the potentiating cohabitation of these mutually exclusive parameters founded on some still to be discovered law of the bedrock disease. But what if I managed to cure myself of a craving for or, more to the point, belief in a craving for the rocks yet found myself still prone to excruciating humiliation coming hot on the heels of invidious comparison with every senior colleague in and out of sight? Then—then, nothing. For the rocks were still and forever the core of my existence and whatever managed to go on once that craving for the core was dead could not possibly matter in the least for I would no longer be mattering in the least. So I was decreeing here and now, there and then, and once and for all, that craving—authentic craving, that is—CRAV-ING—AUTHENTIC CRAVING, that is—FOR THE ROCKS—DID NOT MAKE USE NOR HAD IT EVER MADE USE OF EXCRU-CIATING REPROBATING HUMILIATION FROM SENIOR COL-LEAGUES, OR FROM JUNIOR COLLEAGUES INSTANTANE-OUSLY METAMORPHOSING THROUGH THE SAME FOUL TACTIC INTO SENIOR COLLEAGUES, AS A SHADOW FOOT-HOLD in the real world TO WHICH, no matter how much spattered and befouled with bacchanalian ooze, no matter how much spewed forth as incompatible with—downright detrimental in perpetuity to— the exalted aims of such colleagues and their boom town clientela TO WHICH, for purposes of further humiliating reprobation and excrucia-tion, that is, rehabilitation as merciless judgment but in the grandest manner, TO WHICH IT—AUTHENTIC CRAVING—COULD AL-WAYS COUNT ON RETURNING. Here and now, before I plum-meted once again into the lukewarm pool of undulating rock flesh, I was proclaiming that craving—authentic craving—for that flesh flexed its wings, unsheathed its tail, in no mangled shadow of vindictive rehabilitation—was padded with no prospect of an eternal return—laid itself bare amid no frantic covert calculation of the probability of catching the 9:07 trolley back to the mainland—was pursued—de-ployed—unfurled—in full knowledge of the unknowability of conse-quences and fatuity of posthumous footholds—in full guttling pig-snouted impatience for the smell of its own wild writhing caught in the act of commingling with unspeakable forms.

At any rate, here she was again, back at my side, preventing me from advancing, even if craving for the rocks had its roots in the paradigmatic shadow cast by the swarthy and rugose trunk of the doctor yoked to the horns of his own kind—a shadow that managed to resound the syllable of eternal damnation out among the farthest constellations—even if this craving for the slime and shit that clogged their crannies had its impossible beginnings in my helpless rage at the involuntary—INVOLUNTARY—raging envy induced in her likes by the likes of the doctor and his likes—there was no going back to the source at this late date in the name of purification, in the name of cure. For craving for the rocks and the slimy shit shelvelike they descended gently toward me on its way to the foaming sea, or, if you prefer, phobic repudiation of the likes of her and the doctor—who went on refusing at all cost to be rocks—had advanced too too far beyond its incunabula— had become festooned with too too many accessories redolent—nay downright constitutive—of if not a more advanced than certainly a less decomposable congeries of unspeakable cross-purposes.

In short, I could in no way trace my path to the rocks— depending on the day, the minute, this or that particular ribbon of dust haphazardly and halfheartedly scattered to bring me face to face or rump to rump with the forbidden contours—for the life of me I could not trace it back to, say, the good doctor or his brats in their Sunday best or to her scalding upsurges of martyred envy.

Having sprung from nowhere deep within, it had—my craving for the rocks—my path to that craving—no overt connection even with the rocks themselves. I turned to her, still there, still waiting, made a gesture to signal ridicule of this stance of her waiting or of its seeming indefatigability, at which out of the blue she began to weep: I didn't understand for how could my ridiculing gesture be construed as cruel, or rather, such was the cruelty charily allotted one admitting and celebrating his impotence. For with all my heart and soul I took the coerciveness of her waiting, which nevertheless in my saner moments even I recognized to be nothing more than a sullen and torpid refusal to go, for the towering strength of unswerving ulterior purpose, and I liked it that way: Call it then another foothold whence to deliver myself, comfortably overshadowed, up to the rocks. Even if it appeared as if she would never budge again and even if she stood blatantly in the way of my going still I couldn't help—hadn't stopped—continuing to crave such footholds as shadows and shadows as footholds to which I might—must—consider myself doomed—with of course all the obligatory kicking against the having—to return. In the large I was surrendering to the edict of her posture—Didn't she see?—as well as to that not so much latent as visibly pregnant in the lily-white good citizenship of the doctor's retreating buttocks—in unison declaring that I must forsake the silliness of the rocks at last and consecrate myself to the more serious pursuit of making a name for myself—in the company. What company? But at the same time time I had to admit that my ridiculing mimicry of her stance—her posture—was not just a celebration of her influence but an outpouring of rage that it should manage to extend so far as to attempt to interfere with my freedom to choose, rocks or no rocks. How dare she connive to abolish the future—the only conceivable future, that bloodily extrusible from the hindquarters of a craving for the rocks—through mere hysterical animosity prompted by the envy of incomprehension? Immediately understanding she shrugged: It's not envy of the doctor that drives me to this point. And in this way she constricted to its pinpoint of spiritual penury a horizon of expectation ascribing global significance to what was after all a mere morsel among billions equivalently caparisoned to gall her with all she had been made to lack through galling connection with me. All of a sudden she murmured, Do you like the north face of your rocks or the west, gently, completely without rancor. And this gentleness tormented me even more than the shrug, which had managed without the least effort to consign the gravamen of my exasperation, through failure to pinpoint the gravamen of her own, to the lowest depths of insignificance. For here she was beautifully and transparently changing the subject in supreme and martyred deference, others might say abasement, to nothing more than my meaningless predilection for meaningless predilections, absurdly fine distinctions without any ground in being, and in which process of absurd and meaningless distinction-making she was, *as ever*, trying to share. The rock faces *meant* for me therefore she was all eagerness to agree that, yes, they must in all likelihood be of the same monumental significance to not merely her but anyone with eyes to ogle and a snout to snort, of course managing discreetly to omit, of course, all this according to the strictures of a pizzle-brandishing despotism simply and starkly incapable of remaining for too long alone with what was fabled through its own inexorable dissemination to have absorbed its attention to the exclusion of all else.

I was moved by her effort but not grateful for it. She could never begin to understand that I was unable to share the rocks, dump them into some caldron of hearty consensual stew. Her interest, however forced, however fantasmatic, threatened them with a density to which they were not at all ready to accede. Truly I had to escape her. You have an ache in your groin for the goats, she said with a resigned smile. I had to get away not so much from her as from the unmasterable comportment of which her presence was now an unrelenting reminder. I muttered something to the effect that for as long as I could remember I had not been able to conceive of myself not loving the mineral world, especially when on the threshold of acceding to the vegetable or animal, and if this love must involve unspeakable abasement before the unimpeded undulation of surfaces rapidly replenished, though over an ever-changing periodicity, with hair-clogged crevices, then so be it, I had no choice but to confront the challenge, as the politicians say. I told her she should be relieved, though this might have been just murky rhetoric, that I was not indeed forcing her to compete with a goat, with whose attributes hers conceivably could be compared. For there was no conceiving the rocks much less their attributes and so no conceiving a comparison of hers to theirs. So I was not preferring to her anything remotely conceivable, especially not by senior colleagues to whose innuendo she was, I knew, particularly susceptible. At the same time I knew I was foxily downplaying whatever violence of upgush I was accustomed, in the vicinity of the rocks, to sanction, and this all in the name of vigilance and against the probability of repercussion for in spite of herself she ended up always attacking the slightest sign of vitality as if it stank of prankish defiance or worse, massively recoiling from, all things considered, its essentially ghostly manifestations, as if each was an ever-widening wounding interrogation of her own capacity to experience the same. For a second, no more, I thought of regaling her with other details, rock-face details, only what point would there be and at this late date in our union getting myself addicted to making her continued existence contingent—as some other's ought to be—should have been—contingent, the other I was desperately seeking—on the multeity of a craving doomed—if, that is, that existence—some other's—was indeed to continue—to an incremental scandalousness.

This was why I was obliged to leave her or at least this was what the story, forever on the lookout for its own unearned opportunities for meaning, was now telling me, namely, that since she like any healthy being existed once for all as I did not there was no possibility of my stitching together a continued existence for myself based second by second, minute by minute, increment by increment, on hers, miraculously warped into a function of some shocked but sober—second by second, minute by minute, increment by increment—reconstruction of a scandalousness whose diffusion I must never allow myself to hope to begin to tire of promoting since promotion was in behalf of nothing less than—continued existence.

What did I expect from the contingent some other—the confessor—I sought and did not know I sought, this one far more than a pretext for thoughts and who though causing pain or rather directing me mercilessly toward pain's way of encroachment must reveal how to induce the thoughts that smother pain before pain itself smothers? Was there any self-respecting confessor agreeable to all this? Far from her at last I was struck first by the dazzling high contrast among various rock elements: Only within the domain—the realm—of the rocks were, it seemed, such contrasts, collisions, clashes, and collocations possible, more than possible, necessary and uniquely capable of founding a newer concept of unity. Here—and here only NO NO NO—here and NO only here—Was this the story once again parasitizing my hard work?—jagged fissures clogged with grass, moss, and fungi of the most unregenerate and unprepossessing varieties cohabited wildly and in harmony with unblemished tracts of a faintly undulating exquisitely textured fleshliness to which—to whom—such crevices, such agglomerations of the kinky, the ragged, and the clogged, could only be anathema and yet, miraculously, were not, though the very next moment this harmony proved completely fictive as blemished fissures and unblemished tracts went their separate ways smarting and ravaged.

I caught a passing glimpse of a goat hopping over a puddle. It seemed that for others—for another—that other—this other, if, that is, the goat or such a goat should turn out to be the very other I was all along seeking and still seeking even if just sprung fully-formed from the forehead of her failure to utter the right questions, perpetuate the unresolvability of certain incrementally expanding scandals, accommodate my rages, cosmetize my inherent sense of abasement into the acme of self-esteem—it seemed, then, for this other hopping so lightly over a wind-tinted puddle, now my other, at last, that the very clashes, collisions, contrasts, collocations, and wild juxtapositions of outlandish harmony that set me writhing—gnashing—with desire—with craving—but for what—for what—if not the fissures and smoothly undulating tracts of unreclaimed and unblemished self-sufficiency, union of tracts and fissures, disjunction of same, their dysfunction as byproduct of their disjunction, one's unconsciousness of the other, one's unconsciousness of the other's consciousness of its other, one's consciousness of the other's unconsciousness of its other, one's unconsciousness of the other's unconsciousness of its other, one's sly consciousness of the other's consciousness or unconsciousness of its other—it seemed then for this lithe, supple, and hopping other the very clashes and collisions of . . . secondary sexual characters that set me writhing—gnashing—gnawing—could never advance beyond the status of mere fact, brute given, and under any circumstances however conducive to frenzy be brooded over, exploratorily fingered as capable of inducing benumbed fascination on the grandest scale. This, at any rate, was what I expected from my confessor. From the way he hopped or skipped it was clear he would make a very good one. Only at the raggd behest of clients such as I would he—the being forever sprung from the forehead of her failure to conform to my unreasonable expectations—manage to distinguish these secondary sexuals one from the other and from the background into which, for one of his ilk, they always tended to subside. And yet my confessor's failure to make fine distinctions where for me all was so excruciatedly distinguishable must never be laid at the doorstep of his obtuseness. Obtuseness it was not, nor could it ever be. In fact from my perspective it was more on the order of blessedness, sheer sublime ease in the ways of sidestepping those ways of the world that lead only to trouble. From the way he hopped and, once done, refrained from hopping, it was clear he had managed, as every self-respecting confessor should but rarely does, to transcend without ever having wallowed in or endured and, best of all, without feeling inculpated and bereft for not having done so that psychosexual stage where the world appears no better than an abomination of opposites and oppositions that must at all cost be reconciled—impossibly—since concurrent with the abomination's emergence is a craving for perpetuation as nothing less than opportunity unparalleled for delirious misinterpretation of, that is to say, excruciated abasement before, its every upsurge.

He was gone soon enough, taking the puddle with him, no one around, only I. The rocks gleamed: they gleamed as I never remembered them gleaming. Vanished conjunction of goat and wind-tinted puddle cast them in a new light. So here, in this new light, was a golden opportunity to rehabilitate myself without benefit of clergy, make her proud of me at last even if she could never be as proud *of* me as she was *for* the good doctor. Here, then, was a golden opportunity to abjure the reality, or at least the density, of the craving, the hunger, the desire. Exalted by this new light who's to say I couldn't, by tailoring my movements, expressions—my very stance—to a certain standard, that incarnated, for example by the good doctor—become—at least in the eyes of others though no other eyes in sight—a mere everything I was not, in other words, everything worth becoming. It seemed to me I could best begin becoming all I was not by hesitating . . . about letting it be known that I, that is to say, the craving, that is to the say, the symptom, that is to say, the desire—in short, I began to entertain reservations about letting it be known, even to myself, that as far as the rocks were concerned . . . But the symptom—the craving—the hunger had no scruples about having absolutely no truck with such reservations and was way ahead of those reservations—far far ahead—in rapaciously inventorying all the bric-a-brac—fissures, hairs, fungi, flowers, streaks of rust, lapilli, mofettes, upthrusts of sun-hardened clay—that might contribute or be made to contribute to its superfetation. It—the hunger—symptom—desire—craving—was already—had long been—in sight of, more than in sight of, in communion with, every conceivable jagged edge and undulating crag hours and miles before I even began thinking of setting the wheels of apostasy in motion. The craving—the symptom—the hunger—had already shored up a handsome store of percepts and qualia well before I began even tentatively to entertain the possibility of denying any susceptibility of eyes, ears, nostrils, fingertips, to the objects responsible. In short, I was far behind the rapid-fire voracity—intelligence—of the craving. But I consoled myself, tried to console myself, to locate a self to console with the reminder that the craving had every chance of becoming an authentic vocation and the aim of that vocation not, as the most commonplace rumor would have it, to transform chaos into order but rather magnify to the point of blinding unbearability some sector—though most definitely not cross-sectional, most definitely not representative—of that chaos and thereby preserve its—the chaos's—purity caught in the act of ghastly spontaneity.

All of a sudden I was terrified of the inappropriateness of such a thought—of its scandalousness—almost as if I had seen fit to throw out my buttocks in the businest of thoroughfares. But a thought about converting craving into vocation—obstacle into opportunity, as the sages would have it—was hardly as inappropriate as all that. I needed more than anything, at least for the moment, to play back the thought *precisely as thought* to assay its commensurateness with the context. Yet here I was attempting to play it back as if an enacted movement, a photo-finish high-wire acrobatic. I recruited all of my movable members for the purpose of reenactment though without success. The thought, threatening to give me away for good, was unreenactable. I had to play back the thought to determine if it had managed to betray me amid so much sunbaked calm. I had to play it back, quickly, quickly, quickly. So busily I went on trying to play back the thought—to catch it in the very act of mocking me as if for all that it was a gesture with a life of its own—until I realized . . . here again I was doing it. Here again. Doing it: Transporting a thought, T", from its true domain into one alien, that the goats or of the rocks, and all in the name of some notorious cento of butt-ends that was to serve ultimately as my story. Here I was daring this thought, T", connected with some long-buried and frightful gesture of long ago, to bare its essence through a frantic striving to resist deformation—and all this under conditions of the heaviest nocturnal surveillance—into thought T^3, connected now with some thought [about converting craving into authentic vocation] striving to deck itself out in the finery of gesture so that thought's essence—T"'s or T^3's—T"'s *as*T^3's—might be preserved. I was giving it, this thought, this T", its only chance to prove itself—to prove it had an essence—a soul—

a core—a nisus of blinding immortality—for how can anything know anything else has an essence unless the latter manages to get itself caught at first hand and up close in the very act of resisting deformation of that essence—soul—core—nisus. Clearly this thought, T", did not belong here. For T" was *about* a scandalous, an obscene, gesture. And there had been nothing scandalous or inappropriate about a thought that dreamed of turning craving into vocation aside from the fact that this dreaming thought was a thought and not a gesture, scandalously obscene or otherwise. So T" could hardly be about this dreaming thought. And so my worry about the scandalousness—the inappropriateness—of the dreaming thought had been fake—a pretense—fabricated solely to plausibilize application of T", originally, no doubt, about some fart-festooned buttock-thrusting—application—adhesion—of T" to its—the dreaming thought's—waffled surface and, by extension, to the surface of a new context, the context of this story of my connection to the rocks and to the goat. Long ago, in the context conducive to that farting and the buttock-thrusting to which T" had been rightfully and righteously applied, it had doubtless been appropriate to play them back, the farting and the buttock-thrusting, in the hope—as was so eloquently enshrined within the thought, T", itself—of isolating specifically ghastly moments of too virulent self-revelation. For that gesture of long ago—that fart-festooned buttock-thrusting—had doubtless been witnessed by all or by some among which some were some who had never taken in the least kindly to its progenitor. Only now thought T" was being applied not to the same or another gesture of equivalent tone color but—to another thought—about craving as vocation—this surrogate being limply made to ape the highly conspicuous character of the gesture it refused to become so that T", obliged to make itself useful at last in contributing a few goosefeathers to the eiderdown of my story, might—as T^3—not be lost forever.

But I was doing the thought a favor, I kept telling myself, offering it, T", that is, an opportunity to stretch and preserve its essence through transmogrification into T^3. The original gesture—the fart-festooned buttock-thrusting—against which T" had been applied—like a poultice—was, after all, nothing more than an expendable contingency better off superseded by my dreaming thought—the new and rightful target of T"'s—now T^3's—manly favors. I was giving T" a chance to preserve its essence. And what was the essence—the core—the burning nisus—of this thought assuming that over heavy nocturnal surveillance it had successfully survived transplantation from its original domain, where buttock-thrusting festooned with feverish farts reigned semi-supreme, to this, where halfhearted knock-kneed zeal to see craving strut in vocation's borrowed finery waned infirm? Its essence had something and everything to do with playing back outlay, whether outlay was thought, gesture, excrement, to ascertain whether it, namely, T" now T^3, had revealed too much *its*, namely, outlay's essence—with self-emanation of any and every kind always involving the risk of incriminating self-exposure—with self-emanation, whether word or thought or gesture or semen or piss—as a potentially—an assuredly— devastating loss of substantive self. And perhaps the preoccupation with the risk of self-exposure, that is, with looking like a blooming horse's ass in the eyes of the other blooming horse's asses, was a mere and welcome distraction from the more dangerous, the more terrifying, because more incurable and irretrievable, loss—dying away—of primal self through self-emanation. And so, through its successful transport from the old context, where it had triumphantly applied, to the new, this, of the rocks and goats, where it most definitively did not apply, at least at first, for how could a thought, namely T", about the terrifying risks of self-emanation out in the world apply—be made to apply—to some other thought never—as is rightly the case for all thoughts— strictly speaking expended except internally—through its successful transport the thought, namely T", now T^3, had undergone and passed with flying colors the acid test of its capacity to *bear essence*—to conserve core and nisus and soul over incalculable distances. In the ostensible absence of a pretext for the exercise of its essence—for what did the essence of T" have to do with my dreaming thought—with any dreaming thought—T" had been born and made, after all, to wrestle with the angel of risk-laden self-emanations, of flamboyantly obscene gestures—in the absence of ostensible pretext for the exercise of its essence the essence of T", now the essence of T^3, had ended up fulgurating all the more unforgettably. Through its transport from context A, where it had reigned triumphant, to context B, where it simply didn't apply, T" had discovered and recovered its essence—its core—its flaming nisus—its burning heart—comprising the monumental revelation that THOUGHT, albeit in this case initially and gratuitously wrenched—by T" as T^3—into merely seeming so—IS IN FACT but a special case of—perhaps the key to—SELF-EMANATION and an OUTLAY as GLARING as gesture, scream, semen, piss, shit EVEN IF—PRECISELY BECAUSE—this emanation is forever CONFINED TO THE PARIES OF THE SELF. The successful transport of T", initially, in context A, about the crying need to play back some ignominious gesture lest it spill too many unflattering beans, to context B, where, as T^3, it had something to say about the thoroughly innocuous thought of conflating craving and vocation, had effected the poeticization of that conflating thought—its shift from innocuous to ignominious—and of all thought. Thanks to the successful sea- or sex change of T" into T^3, thought could no longer be deemed consigned to internal circulation only, outside the pale of the terrifyingly bracing risks of self-emanation. T" as T^3 had solemnly, or not so solemnly, decreed thought qua thought—as much as gesture, grimace, movement, outcry, fart, shit, sweat, blood, and sand—in perpetual danger of devastating barrier-breaking visibility. And my story had moved on a little further.

One rock face suddenly stuck out with particular force of beauty. In response, with unusually decisive speed I elaborated a scenario of prostration so full-bodied and so vile clearly one intent on such a course could not be allowed in the vicinity of women and children. At the same time I was convinced if only this rock face—of course jagged with tiny hair-clogged fissures but with the hairs combed at an angle of thirty degrees to the undulating flesh—would have the decency to dip or disappear then—then—then—I would be free at last not simply of this face or that or of all rocks but of craving itself. Yet the moment this particular specimen was, due to my own divagations, lost to sight freedom—from this particular specimen, from rocks in general, from craving—no longer had any meaning. Incised by the loss, I was incapable of striving whether toward new rock faces or a vocation or a craving antidotal to that which for so long had been making a vocation of hurling me crashing against them or some being, some thing, willing to serve as repository for a telling of all the scandalous outcomes of striving, that is, abasement, now dead and unburied.

Now that the rock face in question—though wasn't every rock face for the duration of its season the rock face in question—had dipped out of sight there could be no subsequent success big enough to indemnify me for its loss, the most telling of all losses, unless by no means was it the most telling of all losses, rather the most NO among the most supremely trivial of losses and in its triviality su NO prem NO NO supremely NO *rather* prophetic of far greater losses to come and therefore a first step on my road to narcotization to loss. I was just about to lick one of the hair-clogged fissures, one of the seams, with my now burning tongue when it struck me dumb that I had done it again, that is, induced a connectedness between two thoughts, both from another context yet transplanted for comminglement in this so that the cento of butt-ends that was the story, my story, might proceed toward its unnatural conclusion since all conclusions are unnatural: arbitrary, gratuitous, meaning-mucked. Two thoughts from another planet, another universe, totally unconnected, sundered perhaps from infancy or well before, had been "reunited," condemned, that is, to flow each into the other's slime. Thought T^m, which may once in Aleppo or nearby have concerned my relation to her, was now constrained to apply to that straining to subsist between me and a particular rock face. Having for so long perceived her to be the cause and source of all my ills I had understandably wished her away so all ills could vanish in tandem. Such a thought, namely T^m, sublimely plausible in its home context, had now been wrenched into applying to some state of affairs totally incompatible with its lambent core in the feeble flustered hope that triumphant survival would simultaneously flash forth and reveal the virulent and indestructible essence at the core of its core. The thought, T^m, now applied, as T^n, to a given rock face. Had I ever hoped to be rid of rock faces as I had forever hoped to be rid of her? Impossible. Yet I had hoped, and not so long before, to be rid of a particular rock face so that incommoding desire—craving—hunger—for that face could be obliterated in tandem. So the two contents, old and new, were not as incompatible as all that. At any rate, the core—the essence of transplanted thought T^m as T^n—something along the lines of—to the effect that—if only I were free of her, I mean particular rock face R, then I would be free of this craving for rock face R, for all rock faces R, for all things R and not R—the core and essence of T^m as T^n was its transliteration of a wish [by getting rid of X to get rid of the ills occasioned by X] using the alphabet of cravings and not of ills. Getting—being—rid of rock face R I hoped to be rid of a craving for R: Another facet of T^m as T^n's essence—core—fulgurating heart of darkness—was its willful confusion of external absence with internal disappearance, RESULTING in the poeticization of infirmity as infantilism recaptured. Getting—being—rid of rock face R I hoped to be rid of a craving for R, for all rock faces R, for all things R, and rid as well of craving itself. A final facet of T^m as T^n's essence—core—fulgurating heart of light: its surrender to overwhelming afterthoughts [. . . for all rock faces R, for all things R, . .], the aggrandizing flourish of annihilation possible only on the level of a telling; stratagem as well for BOTH masking the essential craving—first, last and always a craving for the rocks—by presenting it as one—and a measly one—among many in an infinitely expanding series AND transcending its—the craving's—degrading embodiment of just another not quite name brand of humanness.

Being suddenly free of rock face R had been equivalent to its being lost from—dipped out of—sight. This equivalence—willful confusion of external absence with internal disappearance—was the seam, the swivel, the pivot, that had allowed thought T^m as T^n to be yoked to another similarly transplanted from a home context forever lost. The rock face's being lost to sight was the story's unsolicited deference to the fulfillment of a wish—to a psychic hunger—satisfied, compliments of its—the story's—ingenuity, as a vicissitude of topography, of itinerary. The story—my story—my cento of butt-ends—had instantaneously and eagerly agreed to treat a mere dipping out of sight—a being lost to sight—this vicissitude of topography—as an authentic ontologic obliteration adequate to an equally authentic psychic upheaval, with the obligatory ration of jeremiads, dereistic descents into helplessness, and forthright refusals to keep on trucking or fucking thrown in for good measure. So the rock face, R, had been lost—its loss successfully managed—topographically, psychically: Here was where T^o came in, applied now to the psychic/topographic loss of rock face R but within its home context doubtless connected with that of some authentic fetish never to be retrieved. T^o, supremely applicable to such a loss, had been roughly wrenched toward applicability to the loss here of some godforsaken shard which, for all practical purposes, the very urgent need to find a home for its—T^o's—essence had sleekly and singlehandedly fabricated from scratch. The proclamation of hopeless craving *for* and almost petulant refusal to go on malfunctioning at the same rate of inefficiency *without* impossible indemnification for loss, supremely and intolerably poignant as it may have been within T^o's true domain, loss's authentic home, when now foisted off on a state of affairs—trumped-up decline and fall of some superannuated boulder—that could by no stretch of the gut be perceived as warranting the wayward intensity worthy of a fetish, totem, heirloom, swag, was suddenly better than poignant, was farcically forthright in its demonstration of how to keep a story moving through on-the-spot recruitment of nothing less than—poignancy. T^o, supremely applicable, then, to authentic loss of authentic gewgaw in its home domain, had been perpetrated on what was only at the last minute trotted out as same purely so that T^o as T^p might interlock with T^m as T^n and thereby keep the story as cento of butt-ends coming full speed ahead. No thought worth the name wanting to be adequate to, in other words, swallowed up by, its occasion, T^o had grabbed its chance for the resurrection of an essence already fading fast from too much plausibility with respect to the state of affairs initially provoking it: the more inappropriate the present pretext the better if that essence, fading ever faster, was to show forth reconstituted as the radiographically precise schema of itself. At the same moment story had pounced on *its* chance for additional headway, however modest. T^o then as T^p. T^m and T^o, then, as T^n and T^p, butt-ends recruited to the cento that was the story—my story—of the rocks and the goats or of the space between these two dia NO diame NO diametrically opposed modes of becoming and remaining primordial incarnated by equally though differently lovable subspecies of the same demiurge singlehandedly responsible for the infinite variety of my afflictions. Two incompatible thoughts—incompatible first with their new context and then with each other—had been seamed and soldered. Though what I was just now discovering, dreaded discovering, was that no two thoughts are incompatible, no thoughts are incompatible, and that in actual fact NO NO NO it NO was NO

PRECISELY IN THE DOMAIN NO NO NO NO OF THE CENTO that thoughts apparently incompatible discover their essential and ineluctable affinity. In the domain of the story as cento and of cento as story they cease, these thoughts, no matter where they hail from, their inconsolable puling as exiled butt-ends, so that what was by hostile spectators and senior colleagues initially perceived to be an imposed and gratuitous juxtaposition of incompossibles alarmingly free of reason and measure is rapidly discovered to be in fact a deliriously festive homecoming, the almost tautologic accrual of like onto like, accretion of like deep within the heart of like, attraction of like fiercely unto like, renewal of too long buried affinity, resumption of too long dissimulated homology.

I had no choice but to give thanks unto the story for transmog- rifying the psychic upheaval inseparable from threatened obliteration of the beloved, whoever and whatever that was, into a story line, the line of vanishing topography, quirk of itinerary. Only within the domain, that is to say, the ruins of the story was obliteration of the craved object— whatever that was—equivalent to its temporary and fortuitous eclipse compliments of landscapely ups and downs.

I gave thanks unto the story and applauded its "marvelous ingenuity." For the transmogrification of *destruction of the beloved object*—the prize possession priceless beyond price—into an undulating disappearance from sight and vice-versa had been among its most indecipherable ploys for keeping itself—and me in tandem—going— ploy as well as ironical and bold unconcealment of an impish sleight-of- hand—poverty's incomparable sleight-of-hand in recruiting as plausible substitute for destruction—ontologic obliteration—that never could have been conceived within the limits of story event—situation—pertur- bation—a bona fide story event—a topographic vicissitude—undergo- able by those limits. The story had managed to transform beloved object's disappearance among the hills and hollows of my route into a destruction, thereby poeticizing that disappearance. Calling on an in- fantile mode of apprehension and cognition, story had managed to recapture, that is, poeticize, disappearance, in its essence forever and for everyone—destruction. I moved on. A few of the rocks were listening, especially hard. But as I bore down upon them, or rather, as my desire—hunger—craving, bore down upon them it became clear they were not so much listening as waiting for some other, me or some third, perhaps the very thing or being I was myself waiting for, receptacle— crucible—of all my ignominies—to come forth and look up or look down, notice, at any rate, the listening, their dutiful absorption, their capacity to flawlessly simulate absorption in the babble, spoken or unspoken, of the self-important other. This capacity to simulate mani- fest absorption in the rambling self-proclamation of another had to be valorized either because extremely rare or because there was something to be gained from such a simulation. But what. Maybe the simulation of thralldom distracted them from a more essential thralldom. Suddenly I was afraid the being I sought would turn out to be a mere simulator: I came upon him all of a piece, or rather, there he was, incarnate, as one of a pair uncomfortably seated on what looked like a bench patched together out of the shoddiest rock face detritus and bleached bister by evidently too prolonged immersion in shade and damp. Clearly they were strangers, uncomfortable in proximity, downright hostile, yet doomed to a minimal amenity through some law of consignment, connected with the present universal dearth of such pulvinars, to the same seasidy slab. One was speaking, or trying to speak, to the other— *my* other—of his job, his apartment, his odyssey, his many loves, his loves too few and far between, his appetites, appentencies, and intes- tines—giving the recitation a greater and greater urgency as if in direct panting response to his interlocutor's far too rapidly expanding, well- nigh intolerable, curiosity. Only the other—my other—never looked at the speaker but always beyond, at me, just as once long before he had been hopping beyond the wind-tinted pull of a puddle. Only now it was I trying to get my bearing. He was inviting me to share in his astonished irritation tinged with amusement, the connoisseurial delectation of, in spite of himself, the listener born. His look furnished us with a shared history, a long and fruitful—an impregnable—one. His look reminded me that we had been in this same place at the same time far longer than he and the other, which fact indisputable made it altogether natural for him to be counting so very passionately on that history—breeding a retroactive affinity—to put the other's colossal bad form into context—into bold relief.

I sat down and back but nowhere near them. There was nothing further to do in the name of this new relation to the goat. In the shadow of the other's terrible lapse from propriety, which lapse might conceal or be very much on the verge of revealing a far more serious anomaly—clearly I could look forward to a long reprieve. But from what. Though from what. From what though. From somebody's—his—merciless concentration on my own flaws, my own lapses. I began to bask in the terrible sunlight of high noon, so intense it was, at moments, indistinguishable from darkest shadow. In the shadow of this reprieve—at last, then, I had found a judging shadow all my own, a foothold in the shadow of imminent judgment, but at the moment that shadow was otherwise engaged reprobating yet one more pitiful specimen thereby erogating a puny pitlike peculium of borrowed time among the rocks—in the shadow of this reprieve, I could look forward to the most voluptuous of interims, already begun, its mucous membrane invested with his heartiest thanks for my stolid persistence in a being with no other claim on his gratitude than its stalwart refusal NO to NO be—the slothful impossibility of its becoming—the being of that other denizen of the bench. When I opened my eyes, however, he—in high contrast to whom I had rapidly gotten used to standing out as so inexpugnable a paragon of the better class of emotions—was gone: It was only the puddle goat, my confessor, and I. He was looking hard at me but the look was no longer mitigated by entreaty that I confirm the outrageousness of some unwanted third party. There was a third no longer. Only he and I. Only he, only I. His outrage—his absorption elsewhere—no longer invoked and delimited a space in which to fantasize unimpeded the limitless aggrandizement of my sudden worth. Yet shouldn't I have been glad he was no longer abandoning me to his preoccupation with the other, shortlived source of that worth, equally shortlived. This other gone, I moved from my resting place into what I perceived to be the thick of a fray of rock faces. Immediately he called to me. I don't mean he called to me directly but the artful way in which he made his already diminutive figure dwindle still further spoke volumes whose gist was roughly, For you the rock faces may represent the domain in which to play out your deepest cravings. But what you take for avid response—from their undulations—is a mere muddleheaded preening and primping for inbred revels in which you can never hope to participate and which—the preening and primping—of all things has you least in mind. And so you must finally ask yourself: If in the waning or waxing light they—the rock faces—seem to be veering toward you is it purposefully in the direction of a personal charm loudly latent or a mere tropism triggered by the minute, tenacious, flattering, and—when all is said and done—completely undifferentiated attention with which you follow what you reflect back to them as their trailblazing progress. As I turned to him and at the very moment to solicit clarification I regarded his expression most closely he managed to transform his captious scowl into some thoroughly neutral, absentminded, even well-intentioned yawns. Skipping over a puddle burgeoning in the hollow between two juttings I knew that from where he stood my reflection must be imprisoned in that puddle. Walking off I suspected my shirt, no my head, would be the last to disappear from its callow depths. And I loathed this puddle not merely for its newness to the scene of our relation but for my eager hopefulness triggered by that newness. Clearly, hopping a puddle before his very eyes was not the same as watching one's incomparable mentor-to-be perform that feat. I knew too that from his standpoint—always and forever from his standpoint—I must appear to be walking off with the off-balance optimism and alacrity, missing only knapsack and sneakers, of a superannuated schoolboy. A rounded boulder—not a rock, not a rock face—was parked not far from the puddle: one of its windshielding facets was doing an admirable job of warding off the encroachment of earth and sky. This discovery, all my own, that the windshield was all of being's center of gravity, became a sigh of relief. The goat then was not the fount of all wisdom, of all spiritual density. He had been ousted—at last. By a mere—and magnificent—boulder. This discovery meant nothing less than that until our next interview, though who could say when and if there would be a next interview, I did not have to hold myself in suspension for the frantically desiderated overruling of a prior veto of my continued existence embodied in the captious scowl, or was it the neutral, absentminded, well-intentioned yawns. Overruling, that is, with a kindish word or two. He was coming after me, looked at the rocks, then at me, as if my universally acknowledge privileged relation to their facets offered him a unique and unrepeatable opportunity of ingress. Hounded, I was as incomprehensible to myself as I knew I had to be to my hounder, even if his eagerness of self-absorption made him madly impatient of such incomprehensibility. He wanted to discard it, but how could he, suddenly I was no more than what he failed to distill, from my surface or my depths, of their—surface or depths'—equally enviable relation to the rocks. At other moments, as I strove to meet him head-on, he became not my pursuer—my hounder—but an innocent bystander, if not quite a gory onlooker on the order of the good doctor, gaping with repulsive dismay, his ruby-red lips all everted rubber tire, at being reduced to a mere segment of my vast trajectory. Standing to one side of me he allowed his shambles of a stance to say, There is no existence outside the symptom's upsurge, that is to say, no enlightenment outside the craving. Of course, it was by no means easy, even from a short distance, though ultimately the difficulty had nothing to do with distance, long or short, to determine what his stance was doing, much less saying. First I had to determine and sequester the bassline saying of the stance extrapolating to and from some antediluvian moment of our shared past when it could not have been construed as in any way directed toward me or the scandalousness of my doings—some moment, then, of yet outside that shared past when he had neither divined nor foreboded my existence though who's to say he had ever been completely eviscerated of the awareness now proving to be my undoing—and having determined that substance of bassline saying, that tare, so to speak, to subtract it from the overall saying of the present moment and thereby derive and deduce this present moment's supplement, to wit, There is no existence outside the symptom's . . . no enlightenment outside the craving. I fixed on the celebrated puddle scene, that moment of his puddle hopping when he had been still untainted by our connection. So it was by subtracting its content—the content of hopping stance—from overall present content that I had come up with, There is no existence outside the symptom's hunger. It now seemed as if he had read this adage off the rocks where it was scrawled for all eternity to pore over. He looked hard at me or rather his tail wagged hard as if to emphasize that only through scrupulous analysis of the symptom—the craving—the hunger—the desire—could I ever hope to begin to understand the disturbance event in which he, I, and the rocks were enmeshed. Kicking a little refuse in the direction of his dovegrey dewlap meant that he had absolutely no reluctance about formulating the confusion that must at this very moment be uppermost in my beleaguered skull: No: he did not expect me to burrow in my past. A gob of spit aimed at his own delicate ribs elaborated: That would be barking up the wrong tree, for, in my case, oh how well he knew this, in my case, a special case if ever there was one, to be true to the past was to be true to my marginal status in that past. Didn't I see that entering the past directly, as I expected him to expect me to do, could only mar and rupture whatever remained intact of that status, however marginal. I did not respond. His rump and shoulder blades remained latent, stank of withered timothy. Sticking out my tongue at his slightly bruised poll was my version of outcry, in this case meaning: The rocks are my past and if you had ever bothered to notice my adits thitherwards were always forthright and fearless, never tentative, never furtive. Now that he had outlawed a forthright and fearless trek into the past I could afford to swagger, flaunt a fake reluctance to comply without a fight. He laughed, or rather, his little beard wriggled and his nostrils rawly flared and, again as if reading off an eternal slate, modified his stance to mean and for all to hear: The only way to resolve the symptom, in other words, your very being, is in the domain of the symptom. Even if you wanted to you could never step outside the reality of confrontation/immersion which, for you, is the only reality there is. In other words, though as a matter of principle I am always loath to use other words when these words are at least as good, confrontation/immersion is your primordial mode of being. No help for that. His eyes met mine: I reeled, whether with lust or disgust, I cannot say. Rolling over in the dirt so as to expose his hindquarters he proceeded ably onward and upward toward the light of reason's sleep: Even outside the symptom, i.e., outside craving for the rocks and for their hairy old fissures, his latent teats proclaimed, you are inside, always inside, for this being outside is definable—intelligible—only as a not-being-inside for the merest interim, that is, only as a temporary not-being-inside, in other words, only as a nonbeing, always and only as a nonbeing doomed, alas, to revert subsiding once again to a being-inside-the-craving-as-of-old. Within or without the domain of the rocks you are of the rocks. You are—here his pinbone twitched though I cannot say, *mischievously*, as story syntax would have it—a rock-bottom personality.

What prompted such a diagnosis at this particular juncture? For at this particular juncture nothing particular was taking its course, at least, as far as the rocks and I were concerned. His diagnosis was either belated or premature and the glaring hysteresis of course responsible for its troubling force. His golden rule, at least as far as I could detect: The diagnosis—thought T^m—must not—must never—fall where appropriate. Its out-of-nowhere effect filled me with an overwhelming sense of betrayal, too virulent to be laid solely at the doorstep of diagnosis-content alone. I tried not to focus on betrayal but to imbibe all he had poured forth and was still pouring forth in a series of slogans: Craving or not craving them I was of the rocks. My hiatuses of not-craving could not be equated with the not-craving of others. Mine were not-cravings in unremitting relation to a ubiquitous craving. The rocks and I, with him perhaps thrown in for good measure, comprised a system whose craving-mechanism was localizable in no specific cog or escapement but rather in the optimal dysfunction of the whole. My role was to register difference—difference between this, that, or the other fissure or hair-clogged rent or hairless undulation AND its ideal form—and to effect the transformation of differences—registered deviations—into efferent messages slated for the landscape apprisable and apprised thereby that I, part and parcel of its—the landscape's—perennial perversity, was as susceptible as ever to that perversity—perversity, that is, to the practiced eye.

So close at last to the rocks I no longer felt any desire—craving—for them. For as long as I could remember I had been depriving myself, to say nothing of her and of the little ones with their screaming little rosebud mouths, in order to defray the cost of an ultimate descent upon the rocks. *But as it was turning out*, in the shadow of his hounding, that is, craving for their incorruptible venation, ostensibly compatible only with maximal thrift and self-denial, had now been superseded by a preoccupation with denial for its own sake. At present the little economies were the core of the craving, no longer a craving NO for the NO NO rocks but for NO NO NO the maximization of self-deprivation

This was not true though for a second it had seemed true, a way to go on, with or without the rocks. More NO than NO the craving—the symptom—the NO—he NO had undone me. His pursuit was making me feel despicable. YES: Here, then, is a better way to do on. I felt that if only I could YES rectify my image, shattered YES by the doggedness of his lucidity—and in some unquestionably prepotent handling of a major event or memory of one: I needed to be able to rescue some rock, for example, from the retorsive grip of its congeners. Successful I would have every right to feel myself reinstalled within my own precincts, my own contours. And if I managed to amuse the little ones and render them, as a consequence of my ready wit, stalwart and steadfast, wouldn't such a quiet feat make up for an infinitude of disintegrations exasperated by the high contrast between his muscular lucidity and my torpid flab. An echo resounded from the undulating faces: I cannot be treating you—curing you—outside the emulsion you-rocks-me. To the echo I retorted there was no reason on earth to believe my devastated craving for the rocks and its lucid contempt for that craving were necessarily mutually potentiating: There was every possibility that my craving's tenacious virulence would ultimately undo that contempt. I began to speak to the rocks but like him, telling them that no matter how hard they tried they would never manage to secede from the mechanical system we constituted. I did not want to speak like him, like his echo, like anyone but myself, especially now that so little of that self had managed to resist the leak into nonbeing. But no matter how much I knew myself to be outside being—little more than a web of the words of others—I knew even more strongly—now NO more strongly NO NO NO—now more strongly than ever YES NO—before NO YESNO— MORE STRONGLY THAN EVER BEFORE—that words, that is, the words of others, would somehow always manage to continue coursing through thereby causing me to collide into the momentary and fleeting construction of such unavowable selves, hardly espoused, barely noted, as were subtended by these words: spew-worthy selves yet forever in mesh with my strange torment. So I went on using his words, his words for my craving, his ready words for my belated craving, for what better way to contend with unavowable erithism than to hawk it as another's. I cried out to the goat, the distance between us NO wider NO than NO ever WIDER THAN EVER, but long before I had finished the question, something to do with why he went on pursuing me, I knew it, the question, did not exist to be answered but rather to be docketed as a datum appertaining to yet another moment in the flash-in-the-pan life cycle of the parasite-propositus that was I.

To his face I cried: I was born to feed upon the rock faces, to live off their inexhaustible vitality. All along I had been enumerating my sorrows to distract him from his own too piercing perception of my ever-expanding exploitation of those less mobile. Instead of sneering, as I had expected, he moaned long and loud, which moaning long and loud was his way—I was sure of it: the quiver of his left nostril gave him away—of contributing yet another entry to my overflowing list, to wit, economic deprivation. At first I experienced inexhaustible delight at this sign, so what if from afar, of authentic concern. But then some unlocalizable shiver of the landscape transformed this shred into a snub that provoked—rage without bound. For by adding economic deprivation what had he managed to do but show himself eager to toy with my easily enumerable deficiencies at his leisure thereby goading me through fulsome demonstrations of putative comradeship toward a misguided pursuit of reparation. Was he my friend, this goat, and if so did his friendship extend to the showering of blessings on my pursuit of the rocks? Slowly I made my way toward them even if I was in the midst of them. I had a tendency to make my way toward them even NO especially NO NO ESPECIALLY WHEN NO NO NO in the midst of them. Slowly but steadily I made my upright way toward the midst of them. One, in the middle distance, was of an especial uprightness, of an especial beauty in this purplish ruin of dusk, as if beckoning toward me alone. I did not know if at this very moment I had a desire to visit the rocks but I did know that somewhere in the mechanism it had been computed that such a visit must take place. Forestalling the moment of surrender, delicate for all concerned, I took the long way around, gathering a few ventifacts. Rubbing their abraded edges against my flesh I experienced not a whit of desire, usable desire, that is. Therefore it was prefectly clear: I was immune to the main event—the rock faces. I turned back to see the goat lingering speculatively in the wake of my apparent insusceptibility to the ventifacts. He made a little darting movement toward me, expressing far more clearly NO than if he had put it into words his lofty and categorical skepticism where such insusceptibility as proof of global immunity was concerned. As far as the gently tripping movement of his right front, then left front, leg was concerned my repudiation of the ventifacts simply meant that only the main event—deployment of the blossoming rock faces to most startling effect—would do, though not necessarily handsomely. Descending inevitably on the beautiful upthrusting formation posturing as if for me alone I took heart at the sight of two smaller formations pretending to loiter but posted in fact janissarially on either side of my target. Surely they would protect me from the unknowability, that is to say, the overwhelming violence, of my intentions. Yet once returned, after moving briefly away from the shame induced by their grim fealty, to discover them gone, what was my surprise at the surge of relief followed by yet another surge—of shameless certainty that now, yes now, enter I must. So it was in fact their absence rather than some visible emanation of ostensibly myrmidon-like strength that ultimately prompted. Unless it was the boundless despair at their mysterious departure enhancing the despair driving me into the arms of the rock faces in the first place. Still I walked on, still the goat—my goat—was never far behind, both of us bona fide denizens of the dead sunlight, dead because it had ceased to matter for the incomparable texture of rock faces. I climbed, descended, reascended, stared at the sea, unable to decide, weighed down by fatigue yet deriving a certain pleasure once I took to crawling—noted, I noted, by several straggling bright beasts, second cousins to my gory onlookers, busy sunning themselves—from appearing in their eyes—always in theirs—totally indifferent to the rocks, the rock faces, now positively flagrant in their repudiation of earth, sea, and sky, deriving a certain pleasure—perhaps NO the NO NO greatest GREATEST NO—PERHAPS THE VERY GREATEST PLEASURE OF ALL—from being momentarily, at least in my consciousness of theirs, one of their number, just so long, that is, as I managed to go on mimicking, in other words, creating as much for them as for myself, their absolute and utter indifference to the target of my cravings. Even if in their case, the case of the bright beasts and gory onlookers sunning themselves for all they were worth in a total absence of sun, it was never a question of indifference, absolute or otherwise. For in their case it was a classic case of indifference beyond indifference, of an overpowering failure to conceive of the rock faces, that is, of the rock faces as distinct and distinctly upsurging—as prolapsing into distinctness from an all-encompassing monolith unamenable to anything stinking even imperceptibly of the diacritical flourish. In short, these bright beasts were very much outside the system of craving decreed by him—my goat—my puddle—my confessor—to be the medium par excellence of my rehabilitation. But at the same time their noncraving could not be reduced to the mere obverse of craving as I strove to practice craving. So that what I was ending up mimicking was not in any shape or form even remotely connected with what they must be feeling since, where the rocks were concerned, the bright beasts made it a point without in the least making it a point to feel nothing, nothing at all. So that I was only mimicking, could only mimic, what I thought I saw, in other words, what I desperately wanted to see—the desperation in direct proportion to the unlikelihood—which was acute bafflement attempting halfheartedly and touristically in passing to piece out the muddled meaning purveyed by such an emporium of the emotions as was constituted—for others—by this valley of the rocks AND to determine, localize, plausibilize, the cravings to which its merchandise must pander. Couldn't I say that the craving—my NO craving NO NO—existed only NO and purely NO NO ONLY AND PURELY YES as a pretext for simulating the contrasting and therefore exalted indifference of others? No, I most definitely could not say that— even if the story was eager to parasitize such a perversion of syntax— unless, of course, the mimicry, the simulation, that presumably brought me closer—closer—to them, my bright beasts, my gory onlookers, my haphazard tourists, my goatish senior colleagues, for goatish by and large they surely were, that rendered me well-nigh indistinguishable from their likes, could be construed as a coitus far more total than whatever still awaited me in the vicinity of the rocks. As I walked, crawled, descended, and remounted, I grew more and more intrigued by this creature—this *I*—so skilled at rejecting temptation, nay, totally incapable of comprehending it, much less as temptation. There was, then NO

NO NO NO

NOTHING MORE FASCINATING to my eyes as I skirted the rock faces, themselves no mean sight for sore ones, than NO this NO SELF NO—this shard of self YES—this sliver beatifically incapable of comprehending the craving that was obliterating me, dooming me to loss of her and of the little ones, as well as of any lingering prospect of what the clinicians in their tasteful villas dub without the least trace of irony *a normal life.* So: the sliver of uncomprehending self was far more fascinating than the rock faces themselves. A few more goats were crouched on the sidelines, taking in the scenery, the scene, though no apparent scene to be seen. But I cannot speak, of course, for goatish eyes a-smiling. For one began to smile, too sweetly for my taste, that is, too sweetly to have me as its target and center of gravity, most likely, then, at some remembrance, in other words, some event rendered at last tolerable, in other words unidentifiable, in other words unintelligible to the blunted eyes, ears, nose, and throat of self-love. As I approached or as my shadow encroached she reluctantly began the messy business of effacing the smile. Her initiative met with the others' approval for in a single unison, impressive as a corps de ballet's, they rose to go, their tapping her gently one by one on a pastern meaning, Now you are worthy to travel in our circles.

I laughed to think of myself surrounded with so many goats. What would she have made of it, seeing me so and at the same time so appallingly indifferent to what for some other—interested—party must constitute, I was willing, no, more than willing, to grant, irresistible temptation. I emerged from among the goat folk, to find myself walled off at last from the rocks, not by anything so palpable and gross as a goat tail or fang, rather by the scum that had begun to collect on the surface of the rock faces themselves—the rock faces as phenomenon, as disturbance event—which scumming also constituted a phenomenon though of the second degree. No longer was it a question of whether or not I craved the smooth undulating fissured frequently hairy surfaces. What mattered now was whether or not I would find it in my vitals to resist their absence of solicitation—their monumentally sensuous obliviousness to all forms but their own—and under what circumstances. Or whether I would calmly decide to overcome all impediments—in the form of goats, senior colleagues, gory onlookers, brightish beasts—in other words, all impediments I had myself contrived to elaborate while stalling in their—the rocks'—vicinity—AND enter the naos—the cella—the adytum—the penetralium—the very center of the fane though no welcoming portal or even underpass in sight. What mattered now was whether I would be able at last to muster the strength to gather together and convert into discrete signs all that was not rock and having converted respond to them straight away as the invigorating endorsements of my surrender they in fact were—had to be—could be made even now to be. Or whether, taking a different tack entirely, I would respond to all that was not rock NOT as discrete signs that my time had come to enter, that I was strong and inconspicuous enough to enter [strength and inconspicuousness, reading between the lines of these nonsigns promoted to the status of signs, being directly correlated with the constantly shifting preoccupation of my judges—my shadows—my footholds—among other matters], that my cravings themselves were strong enough to obliterate circumambient obloquy-mongers as so much raster, BUT—taking a different tack entirely—merely as unwieldy and amorphous intimations that this epoch of indecisiveness without end, hopeless pacing back and forth and up and down, would not last forever, would not ultimately cede to similarly endless successor series of facsimile pacings back and forth and up and down against which I—though prime ingredient and pacer—had no and would never have any power to protest. In other words, this *different tack entirely* embodied abutment against the unwashed rump of a phenomenon of the third degree. At any rate, what I needed was a sign, that was clear, and not necessarily from on high, for I was through with signs from on high, I distrusted the on-high. What I needed most was to collide with some object very much down below, though not necessarily hailing from down below, a goat's dropping, a testicle, some incident lowly as an object, some hand-me down redolent of less than regal woe, a pygmy ovine wallowing in the browse of its vomit—some unforeseeable unforeseen collision whence my precarious sense of self inexplicably could be enhanced beyond susceptibility to fortuitous demolition at the hands of the lowliest comer—goriest onlooker—that is to say, constructed instantaneously and momentously from the scratch of a passing connection with some—thing, some recrement of things at odds and immiscible, some embodied reproach to god as infinitely less than man, some object as event, something, anything, dexterous enough to design me anew from my rudiments and concurrently hallucinate the sodality of those rudiments, dazzlingly refurbished, with my fellows'. This is what I needed, the traffic sign I was looking for, to hell with phenomena of the first, second, and third degrees. Immediately I found it: his—the goat's—dewclaw. Then it escaped. It was unclear what this sign—found and gone from the verge of concocting my identity as its sodality with an infinity of homologs differing by less than any preassigned iota driveling down your chin—had intended. Having met up at last with such a sign I despaired of meeting another. And if I happened to would it propel me without further ado into the iniquitous lair or quietly detoxify me of the craving for such a lair or simply attend to perpetuating the anguished pacing up and down and back and forth before the possibility of surrender at last to the solicitations of such a lair?

It was in the throes of my excitement, but over what, over a sign? over its coming? over its having gone? over the certainty that thank heaven I need never look upon its likes again? that I first became certain that I had lost something. I looked around, smelled wrists, scratched groin or what was left of it. I still had my keys to the hovel, driver's license, freemason's identification bracelet, certificate of title to private parts extant, and, most important, the address of Mrs. Rose from the Land of Miracles who over the years had managed to help all those crossed souls who couldn't hold money, liquor, or their head erect; wanted their nature problems stopped; and desperately needed their loved ones back. So what had I—suddenly it came to me: The unforeseeable pygmy event as object—as self-reparational—self-generational—collision—lost long before it was found. The jutting rock faces caressed my ankles, calves, and thighs with their purplish shadow. I turned in the direction of my hounder: He was visible but too far off to have managed to extract some vital force—some precious priceless object—from the depths of one of my pockets or from between two rolls of abdominal fat. I moaned, as I remembered her doing after I struck her, for example. I rushed back in the direction of the faces though forever in their direction, their line of fire, but without any belief in my power to retrieve what was lost or recruit assistance for its retrieval. He was now upon me, sprung from nowhere, just as once, long before, he had sprung the leak of a gigantic puddle while pretending merely to ford what unaccountably had been sprung upon his none-too-available resources. He had seen it all: He beckoned to the others, who formed a semicircle behind him. Yes, I affirmed to him alone, in the lair it happened—I was enjoying myself. And just when I thought they, at his behest, were about to leap forth and claw me to pieces for my transgression they receded. We were alone, he and I, as the gods had all along meant it to be. For the first time I noted he was not a castrato. His pawing of the ground, stomping of his tender feet, the cabbage-and-turnips fetor of his breath—all this spoke volumes: But you did not enter. You abstained. It is only now you are discovering—or speculating about whether it might not be less painful to confess having entered than abstained. For in the case of abstention one is always obliged to explain the circumstances particular to abstention. The last—the bon mot—I deduced from the way he fell over raising his hind legs up into the briny air so I could smell his anus. The hole was fringed with hair but was—I repeat—not a fissure like unto those that at any time of day or night could be found incising the rock faces of my raw youth. It was simply an unprepossessing sluice intermittently flooding him with its own flaunted pride at being able to authorize and empower—overflow—his already considerable native eloquence. Yes, I agreed, drinking deep of the invigorating air whose fragrance rendered my need to be completely in the right far less inexorable, everything is effaced/erased by surrender. He looked to his left, my right. Seeing her advance with the little ones, crawling over the loamy craters and unclaimed pastureland spurned categorically by respectable folk of the senior colleague and gory onlooker variety though more than adequate to our rarissime Sunday jaunts, he smiled and turned back to me, the slight rise of his withers above the wedgelike shoulder blades meaning: A lot of good that brood of blind mouths can do you now. But what he was really saying was: Yes, typically, you learn too late that recounting entry—recounting surrender—may be far less painful than to hem and haw about indefatigable pacing up and down and back and forth and around the ever more remote possibility of surrender, which version of abstention nobody in his or her right mind ever buys, much less respects. Too late you are learning that the shameful—the unavowable— paroxysm occurs not in the den, among the ithyphallic communicants and their furry meandering hieroglyph of fissures spelling ultimate doom, but rather in and among the actual moment of choice, at once a dead space; a hole; a fringe; the most fissurely fissure of them all; an inenarrable liberation from shame, shamefulness, and shamelessness; and an inestimable sop thrown to the story. Too late you have learned— you have learned too late—having already succumbed to abstention—the most shameful of all expedients—and, even worse, to its telling—that report of entry—of surrender—offers a decided advantage over—the confessor who is, as everybody knows, gateway to the rest of clogged and accursed humanity.

Seeing her getting closer and closer and closer with the little ones hanging on for dear life to her little polka-dotted frock—feeling time running out as it always had been but now with a wily purposefulness that was positively demonic, I said, I entered the den down there. I was among the rocks. I was with them, gamboling to the tune of the biggest and the best. He drooped, sadly I knew, for the drooping evidently meant, with or without the convalidation of those gently rising or sloping withers: What you say is a mere—the merest—placeholder for what you do not, cannot, say, namely, that you wandered for hours, years, centuries, debating and debating and debating whether or not to go on counting the hexagonal tiles of the walkway fringed with begonias leading to that most upright and irresistible among the faces. Even if we all know there is no such walkway. I responded as if he had uttered something entirely different and isn't that the *key to communication* as preconized by experts? Then—cavorting and gamboling and singing slightly raucous and out-of-key hosannas to the great god Pan—I was infinitely powerful. He smiled, or rather, his chine—whose peak came down from the withers in an extremely gentle—an almost exquisite— slope—smiled: skeptically. All right, all right—aware that I hadn't much time, that she was, as ever, advancing—only now, then, in the telling, in the telling—all about the shameless havocky gamboling among fissure-clogged denizens of this our deep—only now, in the telling, equidistant between me and you, am I infinitely powerful because allied through the telling with an alien medium, that of the rock faces themselves catching the first rays of the sun or the last of the moon's, against the listener—my listener—my confessor—you—self-styled gateway to the world's anus—world distilled into implacable listener's ball of skeptic and aseptic fire. Yes, now, only now, in the telling, only in the telling, do I discover that the ability to choose, have chosen, overrides what, in this case or any, was chosen, however low, loathsome, slimy, and thereby refutes, for all eternity and beyond, whatever stench, of impotence, of groveling and lazarlike hideousness, of pizzle-spattered prostration emanated—emanates—from it, the medium, the alien medium, in which—by which—through which—the chooser chose at last to find himself. And furthermore, I panted, for I was learning more and more quickly what I needed at last to say even if not quickly enough to keep him from once more lying down on his bony back and sticking his anus in my face as if to say, Stop, liar, stop, it is precisely because my telling is a flying in the face of experience—a contradiction of experience which was after all—yes, I confess—supremely and abominably and unequivocally *abstention*—that I am able to invest that telling and that telling me with so much brawny vindictiveness, vindictiveness against what was not and yet ought at all cost to have been but which, precisely through nonbeing—through being not—allows me to construct myself from scratch which construction—from scratch—from what, in actual fact, precedes scratch by a long shot—which construction—which constructed—infected—telling apotheosizes both teller and told through their very craving for what is—was—not.

He did not appear to understand, being a literal sort of goat. Perhaps I am unfair: His agility in raising forelegs high into the air was certainly a sign, however foulsmelling, that he could function, flourish even, outside the overpopulated kennel of the literal. It could very well embody, that hindlegging and scratching, wholehearted approval for a strategy—my strategy—a telling strategy only just discovering itself to be one and that compliments of collisional collusion with an anus that just so happened to be his, hovering and hairy. So how could I in good conscience reproach him for not applauding what I myself was only just discovering to be worthy of far more than mere applause? Now she was beside me, the little ones hidden among her flounces. They looked a little intimidated, perhaps by the goat, certainly by me, changed irrevocably and no doubt for the worst as a result of my long sojourn among the faces fading. She took my hand, I was most surprised. The goat emitted little cries—as if trying in vain to overleap a three-and-a-half-foot-high fence reinforced with old-fashioned bars designed to slide back and forth, back and forth—to urge her on and emphasize that this was an opportunity far too good to miss and on that account on no account to be missed. She turned to the little ones; at this the little fringe of beard softening an equine turn of jaw wriggled. This meant, unequivocally—even to her, I could see that immediately: Oh don't worry, that gesture—that taking of his hand—at last—is fit for their prying eyes. Don't worry. I was coming, she said, to tell you you must never return to the hovel [she didn't use the word *hovel*, of course; I can't remember what word she used] with or without a job. That we are finished, you and I. But it was at the moment of your emergence from the bog—she called the den of rock faces a bog: I was at once relieved and appalled—that I found you again, so to speak, and more interesting than ever. She conceded but not sheepishly: I had lost interest. One of the biggest among the little ones said, She lost interest, doubtless to soften the monstrousness of what he had just heard by rolling it off his or her own tongue, candy-coated, I was happy to see. As you emerged from that place with which at all cost and to your everlasting credit and since I know you you never wished to be identified in anybody's mind—least of all your own—you were clearly intent only on escape. But then something changed: A new look—of woe—flitted across your features—not your face but your features—hitherto bloated with lust. Could it be you had discovered you might have lost something? She looked at the goat. His chest muscles swelled as if she had every chance of becoming, on the basis of such ingenuity, his star pupil. And the more precious the object in question the more irrevocable the loss. She looked at the children and, for lack of chalk and blackboard, repeated, this time somewhat more sententiously, that is, more gratingly, And the more precious the object the more irrevocable the loss, at which point—

for in this world one thing invariably leads to another—two of the littlest, from sheer terror, or so it appeared to me, a bit nonplused myself, began tearing at each other's clothing and, soon enough, underclothing. This eruption she took for corroboration. The goat was shaking his head up and down—not from side to side—in overwhelmed agreement, as if she very well might—in reward for this proof of a boundless eagerness to please—take it into her neo-Circean head to transmogrify him into a form as quasi-human as my own, or far better, the gory doctor's. Yes, yes, yes, she cried, looking hard at his testicles— as if—as if—as if that into which she was about to translate or had already translated their shaking in unison with the shakes of his head was the very perception she had been groping for all along to explain our relation or its absence—a priceless but by no means stable perception at that, in fact, it was nothing less than the highly labile and inflammable alloy of all wit elicited since Adam and subject therefore to irreversible decomposition if not struck when its iron was hot. Yes, yes, yes—of course—it was only in a desperate effort to stave off the inevitable moment when he must be alone with his loss forever that he about-faced and went back and demanded, I saw him, to have a small flame discreetly trained on the scene of the crime. But so what if it was mere desperation and not heroic forthrightness—as somebody would have us believe—that drove him back to the site of so much undeciphered ignominy tainting not just him but all those connected with him now and forever. For I surrendered to him, as I just explained, Herr Goat, at the moment of his terrified emergence from the bog, I fused with him completely, and not at the moment of his return to the scene of the crime. She was shrieking, kneeled to pick up a pebble. Petrified the goat looked to the little ones—deferred—appealed—to the little ones to protect him from, that is to say, explicate, this sudden outburst. Seeing her consummate rapture reflected in their pasty faces as nothing less than sheer reproachful terror she desisted, good soldier that she always proved in a pinch to be. The pebble fell to earth though I cannot bring myself to allege *with a tinny defeated sound*. She went on as if nothing had happened and nothing had in fact happened: Although in the feeble glow—strangling a sob—you could not quite make out where precisely you had been crouching and gamboling and croaking off-key to the great god Pan. Under my breath I cursed her then interjected: Isn't it intrinsic to a gamboling and a crouching, to say nothing of a wallowing and a groveling and a singing off key, to be unlocalizable, unassignable to a specific site. Even more loudly, the goat my target, I added: The loss sketches somebody's—something's—monstrous slyness—the goat shook its left paw playfully in the vicinity of the dropped pebble—not a being per se but a slyness—a ripple not even of malevolence but of sheer stealth on the scummy surface—though not in the service—of being. A stealth unable to bear the exhilaration of others, not from envy, nor despair, but from a far more primitive physiologic perturbation in the face of alien affect as necessarily a turning away from—a repudiation as annihilation of—its own substance as shadow and shadow as substance. And as a result of that perturbation produced (I take full responsibility) by my momentary and must I point out highly uncharacteristic frolic amid the emasculating alfalfa, lespedeza, timothy, and brome, here I was—am—bereft. But you found it—you found it—what it was you lost. I hated her at that moment. The goat chose the very same moment, among all other moments, to insert its tail into its anus and swirl it around. The orifice was much larger than I had credited it with being, initially. He sighed with relief. Clearly he must be afflicted with hemorrhoids of an especially compelling engorgement. I found it, I found it, I mimicked, with disgust, with hell, in my voice. I turned my back on her and on the little ones, who were clearly suffering from our discord. The goat moved off a certain distance, reflectively, with the full weight of an imposing moral authority concentrated in its haunches. She, for one, looked dumbfounded. I, pointing to the haunches receding: Don't you see what he's trying to tell you. She did not understand. Mimicking again: I found it! I found it! I found it. Self-contained though beside myself: The key, my dear, would have been to lose it—the most precious possession—to lose it forever and ever. For loss of the most precious object of all—two could play at the game of seedy sententiousness—means authentic confrontation with oneself at last—would have surely forced me to reap and suffer the consequences of my actions—my gamboling and crouching—and what more telling consequence than to be adrift—a-drowning—in a puddle of loss. The goat was now returning, his ample lope deprived of any visible moral force for moral force was no longer required. He was as casual now as the shadow-oozing rock faces themselves when engorged with the nectar of high noon. I looked straight at her, sure she must be able to decipher without the slightest difficulty what he had managed to scrawl newly and visibly across his own rib cage. And what did it proclaim but that such a confrontation, authentic or otherwise, indeed would have constituted absolutely nothing essential—a mere excrescence, a by no means indispensable burl of self-stigmatization on the already burl-ravaged bole of my being. It's simple, she said sadly: Was she realizing I had given myself to the faces in a way I never could to her? The disincarnated slyness and stealth you invoke to account for your loss is nothing in fact but your own forgetful frenzy in the face of overwhelming excitement. It was your own pandemonium, a.k.a., the monstrous other, that sought to rob you of your most precious possession: the pandemonium that was an erithism of your very self—your self as erithism—sought to rob you—of you—of the you that would only drag you down and back to me. And to the little ones. I did not answer: this was to her liking. The goat sidled up to her completely entranced. She seemed not to notice: Your frenzy lost you to yourself and tried to furnish you with rebirth in the form of a rock face or hair-clogged fissure at the heart of a rock face. Didn't you once tell me that not loving—craving—the rocks was inconceivable to you from the minute you laid eyes on them. Heard tell of them, I corrected. I ran from her, back to the rock faces, and as I ran both they and I were eaten up first with blazes of sun then leaks of shadow. Hadn't she said this was the moment when she was most interested in me, going back to the rock faces not however to retrieve the lost object, lost forever, lost even before it was known, much less found, but only to stave off the moment of loss, acceptance of loss, acceptance of the merited punishment of loss engineered by the monstrous other that was no one but I at the height of frenzied panic to be at long last too close to the comfort of transmogrification into rock or some other mineral exoskeleton—the monstrous other that was no other than a disembodied stealth on the surface but not in the service of being—some unflensed nonbeing made less in the image of being than to the measure of frenzied dispossession undergone at that golden moment never undergone much less remembered when I had been permitted to swim at long last in the sea of rock faces—some being in fragile and fructive disequilibrium with its nonbeing and forever on the lookout for the split second supremely suited to an insidious gliding between my quivering thighs. Hadn't she loved me best at that moment?

The rocks were panting heavily, aware of their sudden or rather of their gradually mounting importance. She was holding the goat around its neck, trusting to its doctorly skill, allowing it to nuzzle here an armpit, there a breast, forgetting completely the little ones in her entrancement, too deep, much too deep, for the situation ostensibly inducing it. For the situation inducing it had to be my descent into the fiery maw of rock faces for a final confrontation. Only once deep within I remembered she had not been most entranced by the moment of redescent, reactivated here and now. Rather, my "emergence from the bog," etc., had been the spur to—to—I was waiting for the paroxysm, the paroxysm about which he had spoken so beautifully to the extent that he hadn't spoken about it at all nor let anybody else take the words right out of his mouth, as his epigones, no doubt, would have done, those wights that had remained in a semicircle just long enough to establish their sylphlike superfluity. I was waiting for the paroxysm to assault, so what if I was for all practical purposes abstaining still, surely with all eyes upon me ultimately I would stumble on the emancipating act for which I had come so far. For I wanted to be back among her and the little ones, I was not made for other than a so-called normal life bludgeoned by the becalming prolixity of dainty little fixtures. And I could go back only after knowing the paroxysm. I wanted—I needed— to undergo the paroxysm even if I would begin to know it only in a recuperative telling of the doing, or rather, of the having been done to, by the paroxysm, that is, and which up to now, in spite of the urgency of all eyes upon me, wild supplicating calculating—more calculating than supplicating, as befitted the times, alas—had refused to make itself known. But I was still expecting the paroxysm even if I could hope to know it only someday in somebody else's recuperative telling of some- body else's doing as a redoing and undoing. I was still waiting for proof that I had indeed dared and risked all and totally engaged and immersed had finally emerged sufficiently scathed to qualify for that most coveted of all epithets: *Unscathed.* I put my hands over my ears for already I could hear the recuperative telling, but not my telling, of the doing as redoing and undoing, though not my doing as either. She no doubt wanted the storytelling to pay—would expect it to pay—would have me roaming from town to town reminding all available dullwitted fellow-prisoners of that spectacular moment when the sun's last ray falls on by-and-large deaf ears—reminding them that in Aleppo once the very same ray rebounding from rock faces of a certain texture and design goaded them to hurl vindictively and each in turn their notched and gnarled prongs upon my groin and before I knew it . . .

On I went descending for I needed to rectify the first descent even if that first descent in search of my most precious and priceless possession had not been the event managing to endear me to her anew. I needed to render that descent real for only its rectification renders an event real for the first time as its second time's unfolding. Although it is not possible to speak of a first event since the first event, that is, the first descent, not the first descent but the first descent in search of the lost—the most priceless and precious object—had not been an event strictly speaking, for it was only just beginning to exist, or rather, proclaim its failed being now that I was at last owning up to having abused and contused by not planning for it, to having hoped simply to parasitize its inevitability by awaiting the windfall of its inevitable disintegration instead of going out to meet it halfway and head-on in the halfway house, the reputable hospice, of active collaboration in its deployment, however shabby and anticlimactic. Only now could the event be carried through, thanks, say, to my failure to have insisted on a more potent training of a less lambent flame on the hypothesized site of loss. Only now could the event be carried through, so what if only as rectification, indemnification—apotheosis—of a nonexistent predecessor decked out in all the charming, baiting, luring finery of its unlocalizability. I was descending: Event was about to spring. I was quickwitted enough to perceive that, lest the same errors be egregiously perpetrated, I should be scrutinizing every conceivable component of eventual representation now that it—the event—that is, descent into the depths defined by jutting rock faces in pursuit of my most precious and priceless object—was about to hurl itself on my unreadiness. But once again I feared to mar the event—to betray it—by too active collaboration in its birth—by chipping and chiseling away too forthrightly at its latency in the name of an imminent being here and now. Instead I felt inclined, as oh so often in the past, to let it come crashing about me unannounced, imminent no longer, at last ubiquitous and immense. It came, sparing me the excruciating hard labor of having to shape it as the most exquisite among an infinitude of possibilities. Though it had indeed come I was still afraid to offend it by insisting on too major a role in that inferno where it could hardly expect to play the major role itself— there where the burning and scalding of the flab of its lineaments must be the order of the day. I let the flab shrivel and descend, taking default for inevitability. The event had fallen due but once again, as the line-aments lay buried beneath the flab of my discretionary cowardice, not with any inevitability worth writing home about.

I looked back. The goat, dear little creature, was motioning. From a distance I was only first discovering his charms. Each part of his anatomy struck with the force of a logical proposition against which there is no appeal. Why had I never noted the charm close up, in that mellow light of which our concourse now appeared to have been so lavish, so profuse? She nudged him from time to time. Out of fear, I flattered myself, that in my condition, whatever *that* was, I might do myself no little harm and thereby set a bad example sure to haunt the little ones throughout their life. With his right hoof he made a gesture that diminished the density of my troubles for her especial benefit.

Unfortunately, he had been obliged to diminish me in tandem. Yes, I saw it now. This had NO always NO ALWAYS BEEN his loathsome technique: diminution of the supplicant's woes through far less than suboptimal presentation of the supplicant himself—to himself: Stop worrying: Your troubles are small. How can they be anything but small since you are so small. Now I understood *why I had always loathed him* for hadn't he always used the pretext of therapeutic inter-vention, always in the name of concern for my well-being, to reduce me to ashes. Yet wasn't this—hadn't this always been—the essence of goat communication? Yet did I really believe what I had just expounded or proposing it simply to overleap a painful interim? Or had I proposed and expounded knowing full well I didn't believe a word of what I was proposing and expounding and simply so as to savor the ironically inflected acquisition of an observation about the goat kingdom, an observation ultimately, and even proximally, far less about that kingdom than about how universal meaning, whether quasi-, demi-, or semi-universal, always pretends to be stumbled on, that is to say, is generated with the greatest cunning, amid the shabby particulars of somebody's—anybody's—little old story.

Yet she was responding to him, tickling his dewlaps, as if he loved me with the same disinterested love she herself professed to have felt, long before. He called down to me just as I was reaching the site of the loss, now old news, well, maybe not *just* at that moment, maybe he called down a long time before, a long time before I was anywhere near the site—the conception—of loss. But how tell of, that is to say, exalt, his calling down if not as a *calling down at the very moment when . . . ?* How establish yet camouflage that calling down as an indispensable marker on the story's way except as a *calling down at the very moment when . . . ?* At any rate, when he did call down he had much to say, an infinitude, but out of kindness and decency and concern for the little ones falling asleep on their ragged dirty feet limited himself to but a single thing—I know, because immediately he took to twisting his hindlegs one about the other in that way peculiar to goats confronted with the slime of humanity's dregs seeking in vain to retrieve the fixtures of that slime amid the slime which twisting, among goats, can mean *only that single thing* and no other: Know that my response to you, though forever tepid and taunting,—the tepidness *is* the taunting for one as demanding as you—is not a response to you outright but rather tempered—weighted average of a cumulative decline—inflected—by the disquieting effect had—perpetrated—on me by all those who came before and those yet to come, to say nothing of all those with whom I have the misfortune to be already and ineluctably personally and familially acquainted as you are personally and familially acquainted with this young lady and her offspring, yours also, and who, as you must know, tend to breed stalemates—impasses—makeshifts—not only in the relation that subsists between them and us but also and, dare I say it? *a fortiori*, in our relation to ourselves. Whenever I see you it seems I am always at an impasse elsewhere and so it is only natural, though hardly excusable, that I should attempt to make you the cause of my self-dissatisfaction. She, eager to temper such an outburst, not so much out of respect for my feelings as from fear I might exploit—recruit—parasitize it to cripple even further any lingering intentions with regard to reluctant pursuit of a normal life for hadn't I been known to use anything that came to hand as an excuse for semiparalysis?—she beckoned to me, a trifle roughly, a trifle impatiently, as if demanding that I emerge, come up and out and stop all this foolishness, having already wasted enough time and not only my own trying in vain to reconstruct some misbegotten moment, ostensibly golden but only from where I squatted, in the course of which I had had the bright idea not only of redescending in search of what I had lost but of structuring the search—for a prized possession, no less, whose acquaintance I had yet to make—as a redescent: of staging the search—for loss itself—as a rectification of—I knew not what. Very pretty doings, indeed.

I tried to remind myself, to remember and then remind myself, that if her interest in me had reawakened it had been precisely at the moment of emergence from the lair—from the depths—into blinding awareness of loss. So that if only I could find the strength to reemerge interest must be reawakened all over again. But the moment of reemergence was too painful to think about, much less reenact. At the same time it was definitely time to reemerge: I had done enough excavation to last anybody a lifetime. I tried to burrow back into what, for lack of any better, must constitute the privileged moments of my past: moment of emergence from the lair into the blinding awareness that something too precious and too prized had disappeared forever; moment of redescent to retrieve the lost object while remaining all the time fully aware that redescent could only stave off the inevitability of loss. I was exalted by the knowledge that such moments must remain unintelligible to the goat. It gave me an added thrill to be able to subjoin: And his kind. There they were, he and she, still awaiting my reascent. She no longer suspected an unspeakable relation to the goat, to goats in general. But I continued to refuse to mount, I did not want to come back, either to her or to his goaty ministrations. Nothing to say to him. Far too short an interval, this, in which to have accumulated unspeakables sufficient to constitute—to justify—a session. By her meddlesome decree our next session was already well upon us so what if long long before I had managed to accumulate enough butt-ends to smother the underlying unchanging, or unchanging underlying, at any rate insusceptible to the upsurge of a telling. She, for one, did not care if there were not yet enough events—incidents—perturbations—clustered between my going down and coming up to intercede in behalf of an omnipresent terror at being ultimately obliged to locate, hoist, and obtrude the eventless underlying, the underlying eventless: in a word, the substratum of substrata. She wanted me cured, even at the price of my life.

I began my climb: Regulating her steps by its speed, she moved off and away. Reaching the rim of the pit whence one had a spectacular view of the basin and seas beyond, I noted they were gone.

There will be other goats, I told myself, for I had developed, that is to say, at some unlocalizable point in the past I had decided it was time to start developing, an authentic dependence on goats, on panicked misinterpretation of their scarcity of gesture, their movements, impatience of fixity, their dandified protrusion of orifices traditionally left to the bedbugs. The goats were now the only stanchion against which to shore my flights, my excesses, my extremest formulations. The question now became, at least for me, whether a continuing relation with the goat, a goat, goats, would necessarily strengthen me to the point where at some future point of course unspecifiable I could find myself once again entertaining the possibility of seeking her out, or somebody like her, with little ones just like our little ones. But that was thinking too far ahead. That was thinking myself into resumption of loss unspecifiable in front of a site unspecifiable. Over, all over, yet not over, never over when I truly wished it all to be over, over when I no longer wished it to be, for now that I was no longer intimidated by her advance or by the inevitability of goat sessions I found I had something to say, something in the nature of a complaint, perhaps connected with the plumbing in these parts. I had something to say *to all concerned.* Turning full circle I espied her at the edge of a gully, maybe a puddle, his puddle, though without him or the little ones. I was there, visible, but she did not see. For once she was busy elsewhere, no longer preoccupied with my usual deficiencies of presentation. And suddenly I desperately needed a symbiosis with her nonseeing in order to come to my senses, to begin to be. It was only as I prepared to go about traversing the successive layers of ever-widening density peculiar to this nonseeing seeing that I could feel myself slowly coming back to life. Her nonseeing, her unseeing, her almost childlike fixedness elsewhere—but where?—lifted me up and out of my puddle. At last somebody was scratching the surface of the unchanging underlying, the underlying unchanging, that eventless substratum of substrata immune to a telling. At any moment, therefore, the telling must give way.